A Warning

Sometimes love is the most horrifying emotion of all.

This is a story that demonstrates the chilling power of love—how it feeds on the heart, how it consumes the soul, how it forces one to commit the worst of crimes . . .

These things happened in the small town of Thunder Lake, Pennsylvania . . . where a teenage girl loved her boyfriend so much, she broke the laws of nature to keep his love alive . . . where an old man sacrificed his loved ones to satisfy a secret passion . . . and where mothers and fathers, like vampires, drained every last drop of life from their children.

It is the strangest love story ever told. And it is filled with the horrors of death, madness, suicide, and revenge.

The reader has been warned.

Frankenstein's Children

Read the entire haunting trilogy—if you dare . . .

FRANKENSTEIN'S CHILDREN

Book Two:

THE REVENGE

Richard Pierce

B

BERKLEY BOOKS, NEW YORK

FRANKENSTEIN'S CHILDREN: THE REVENGE

A Berkley Book / published by arrangement with
the author

PRINTING HISTORY
Berkley edition / November 1994

ISBN: 0-425-14460-7

BERKLEY®
Berkley Books are published by The Berkley Publishing Group,
200 Madison Avenue, New York, New York 10016.
The name "Berkley" and the "B" logo
are trademarks belonging to the Berkley Publishing Corporation.

PRINTED IN THE UNITED STATES OF AMERICA

10 9 8 7 6 5 4 3 2 1

For my mother and father,
who aren't really monstrous at all.
Thanks for creating me.

Contents

I

The Thing in the Cage

From the diary of Sara Watkins . . .

Six weeks have passed since my boyfriend killed himself.

Every day I wake up wondering if it was all a terrible dream. But then I feel the aching in my heart—the pain, the loss, the guilt—and I know it all really happened.

I keep this torment caged up in my heart. Like a wild animal. It howls and claws at the bars, trying to escape. It haunts me and tortures me—for I am the one who spawned it . . .

And I am the one who must set it free.

In a small town in Pennsylvania, on the farthest edge of Thunder Lake, there stands a tall and ancient house. A run-down Victorian, long past its prime, it rests in a cradle of mountains and mocks the earth itself by refusing to die. High above its weathered rooftop, a solitary tower rises up to defy the heavens. And deep within its bowels, locked in a steel cage in the dusty basement, an unspeakable horror lives and breathes—a child of neither heaven nor earth, but a lost orphan of hell . . .

With a scientific eye, Sara Watkins studied the thing inside the cage.

The creature was unusually quiet today. Crouching down in a corner, it ran its huge fingers back and forth over the stitches that covered its body like a living patchwork quilt. Its limbs hung down, heavy and grotesque, from its lean, bandaged torso. And its long black hair fell down in a tangled mass over its face.

Sara approached the cage slowly. She didn't want to startle the creature.

"Good morning," she whispered.

The thing lifted its head and cast its cold, dead eyes onto Sara. Its black, parched lips opened slowly as it tried to speak . . .

"Sa . . . ra."

An icy chill pierced Sara's soul.

That voice . . . those eyes . . .

The black, matted hair tumbled away, exposing the creature's face. Sara shuddered. The creature's skin was gray and cracked, its features horribly twisted. Its head, neck, and body were laced with scars—deep purple slashes of torn stitches and broken flesh.

Sara sighed in frustration.

She had tried to change the bandages every day, but the thing clawed them away every night—shredding the gauze and tearing the scars that never seemed to heal.

"Sa . . . ra."

Its voice called out to her—a low, unearthly growl that seemed to rip Sara's heart wide open. It frightened and disturbed her . . .

But not as much as those eyes.

Gazing into the creature's eyes was like rubbing salt into the wounds of her heart.

Sara stared at the dead green irises, lost in the empty sockets. The thing never took its eyes off of her. It seemed to study her as much as she studied it—but with eyes more cold and distant than those of any scientist. Sara held the creature's gaze, hoping to see a flicker of *something* . . . anything . . .

Nothing, she thought. No life, no love. Nothing.

But she knew she was being pessimistic. The creature had said her name. It recognized her. There was hope.

"I brought you your breakfast," she said, holding up a ripe red apple and a bowl of oatmeal.

The thing grunted softly and crawled across the floor of the cage.

Sara took a deep breath. She couldn't help being afraid of the thing in the cage. Because she knew it was capable of murder.

She had seen it kill with her own eyes . . .

In the shadows of her mind, she saw the creature standing on the roof of the high school, holding the star quarterback above its head. Moose Morgan screamed and struggled in the creature's arms. Then, Sara watched helplessly as the creature hurled the boy over the edge of the roof—to his death.

"Sa . . . ra."

The memory faded as Sara blinked her eyes and stared at the thing in the cage. He looked sad—and hungry. Bending down, she slid the plastic bowl of oatmeal through the bars and rolled the apple into the cage.

The creature pounced on the apple like a cat. Its cracked lips pulled back to bare a dull white row of teeth. Then, holding the fruit with both hands, it feasted. Chomping. Growling. Devouring the apple whole in three savage bites. It grunted and looked up. Then it crawled to the plastic bowl and plunged its gnarled face into the oatmeal.

Sara watched in horror.

Her cool, rational mind cracked. Her eyes filled with tears, and her heart screamed in pain—not because the thing in the cage was so monstrous and so hideously deformed. Those were just physical deformities she had come to accept.

She was crying because the thing in the cage was her dead boyfriend.

Jessie Frank stood at the top of the basement stairs, listening to Sara's gentle sobbing. She clutched the railing with one hand, a guitar case with the other, and slowly descended the stairs.

Sara was sitting on a countertop in the old cellar kitchen. Her face was buried in her hands.

"Sara," Jessie whispered, "what's wrong? Did something happen?"

Slowly Sara lifted her head and brushed a strand of long blond hair away from her face. Her eyes were red and wet. She cleared her throat. "No," she said wearily. "It's just—you know—it's hard to keep my boyfriend locked up in a cage." She tried to smile.

Jessie set the guitar case on the counter and sighed. "I always said my brother should be locked up," she said. "Well, it looks like I got my wish."

Sara shook her head. "I guess we should be careful what we wish for, huh?"

A dead silence fell over the room.

Because Sara had gotten what she wished for. It was snarling in a cage in the next room.

Josh . . .

Sara looked up at Jessie. As always, she was startled by how much Jessie resembled her dead brother. The same black hair, the same green eyes, the same dark smile.

Josh . . .

A tear trickled down Sara's face. Jessie put her arm around her shoulders and squeezed.

"I wish we hadn't done it, Jessie," she whispered. "I wish we hadn't tried to raise Josh from the dead."

Jessie stroked her hair. "It's nobody's fault, Sara," she said. "If anyone's to blame, it's my family. A bunch of nutcases, going all the way back to the biggest nut of them all, Victor Frankenstein. It was bad enough that he created a monster, but then he passed the secret on to his descendants. What a jerk. I'm telling you, Sara, my whole family is cursed."

Sara bit her lip. "That's exactly what Josh said . . . on the night he jumped from the tower window."

She closed her eyes and saw Josh's mangled body covered with a white sheet.

"That night, when Josh killed himself," Sara said, "I refused to believe it. I was ready to do *anything* to deny the truth. And when Grandfather Frank showed us the journal of Victor Frankenstein, I . . . I . . ."

She burst into tears.

"I know, Sara, I know," Jessie whispered. "We wanted Josh to live again. We didn't care about the consequences."

They both glanced toward the door of the next room and heard a soft growl from the thing in the cage.

"I'm so ashamed," Sara sobbed. "The terrible things we did . . . stealing lab equipment . . . robbing a morgue . . . and getting Eddie to wire up the electrodes. We broke every law in the book. Every law of man and nature and God, you name it. We're just high school kids, for crying out loud. What were we thinking? Why did we do it?"

Sara hid her face in her hands and cried.

"Why did *I* do it?" she whispered.

Jessie took a breath, reached up and lifted Sara's chin. She looked Sara in the eye and said in a calm, clear voice, "You did it because you love him, Sara."

Sara could feel her own heart beating.

"I love him, too," Jessie went on. "He's my only brother. That's why I helped you. I thought we could fix everything, and pretend that Josh never killed himself. We did it for love."

Sara shook her head and sighed. "But look what our love did to him, Jessie," she said. "Our love brought him back to life when he wanted only death. Our love gave him a half-human body and a half-dead mind.

Our love was selfish and cruel and . . ."

"Sara." Jessie put her hand on Sara's arm. Sara looked up and listened to Jessie's words. "Everything you say is true. But it's too late now to change what's happened. For better or worse, our love brought Josh back from the dead. And somewhere, inside that big, ugly monster we created, Josh still loves us."

A single teardrop rolled down Sara's check.

She looked toward the door, her heart breaking as she tried to imagine the suffering that Josh had endured . . .

The torment of his suicide. The terror of waking up in a laboratory. The fear in the eyes of all who saw him. The savagery of the boy he was forced to kill.

And the most painful thing of all . . .

The heartless reaction of his own loved ones.

"Forgive me, Josh," Sara whispered. She touched the gold ring on her finger—the Frank family ring that Josh gave her on the night he killed himself—and she vowed to never abandon him again.

"Look," Jessie said, pointing. "I brought Josh's guitar. Maybe if we put it in the cage with him . . ." She shrugged her shoulders.

Sara frowned. "It's worth a try," she said. "We've got to break through and reach him somehow. I've been playing tapes of Josh's music, and he seems to be responding."

She thought about the love songs Josh had written for her. His music was his life. So dark and haunting, yet filled with tender longing. Like Josh himself.

She looked up at Jessie. "You know, I always dreamed of marrying Josh," she said. "And then you and I could be sisters. That's how I feel about you now, Jess. I feel like I'm part of the family."

"And what a family to get mixed up with!" Jessie scoffed. "Come on, girl. Grab that guitar and knock some sense into that brother of mine."

Sara smiled. She opened the case and pulled out the guitar. Then, arm in arm, the two girls walked to the second room of the cellar—where they had locked up the thing they loved, the thing they feared . . .

The thing in the cage.

A spider hung from a thread, weaving a strand of silk from one steel bar to another. Its web grew stronger as it toiled, its intricate design shimmering in the dull light of the basement. Soon, its trap would be finished, ready to snare its tiny prey. The spider was hungry. Hungry for the lives it would capture and drain.

But the spider was not alone.

A pair of cold, dead eyes were fixed on the eight-legged creature in the corner of the cage. And these eyes were hungry, too.

With large, clumsy hands, the thing in the cage snatched up the spider and thrust it into its mouth. The taste was strange and sweet. The spider's legs wriggled on its tongue.

Then the thing in the cage froze.

The others had come into the room. The girl with hair the color of sunshine. And the girl with hair the color of night.

The creature watched them through the bars. It was afraid they would try to take the spider out of its mouth. It liked the spider. It tickled its tongue.

The blond girl leaned against the bars and spoke.

"Josh. It's me, Sara."

The thing in the cage didn't move.

"Come here, Josh. We brought something for you."

She held up the wooden object. There were strings on it—just like the strands of the spider's web.

Maybe there were more spiders inside.

Crawling slowly toward the front of the cage, the thing held out its huge hands. The girl pushed the guitar sideways through the bars. It fell to the floor.

The thing in the cage stared at the guitar, then looked up at the girl and opened its mouth

The spider wriggled out and crawled down its chin.

The girl screamed.

Startled, the thing in the cage jumped back, away from the guitar. It glared at the girl.

"I'm sorry, Josh," she said. "I didn't mean to scare you."

The creature grunted. Then it turned its tortured eyes to the guitar.

"Music, Josh," she said.

Music . . .

The word sounded familiar to the thing in the cage. It was a word from the creature's past.

Music . . .

It was something like love.

With trembling hands, it reached out for the guitar. Its fingers touched the strings, then plucked them.

Music . . .

A gentle sound vibrated within the wooden object. A beautiful sound—like the sound that came out of the strange little box the girl played for him.

The thing brushed its thick fingers over the guitar strings. A loud strum pierced the silence in the room.

And the thing in the cage remembered . . .

Music . . . that he played when he was alive . . . that he created with his guitar . . . that he felt deep in his heart.

Like love.

The thing in the cage loved music. And it longed to make music once again.

It picked up the guitar and rested it on its lap. Then it pressed its thick fingers on the long neck of the instrument and brushed the string with its other hand.

The sound was muffled and flat.

It didn't sound like music at all.

The thing in the cage strummed the guitar harder and faster. But the only sound it made was ugly and wrong.

Because he himself was ugly and wrong.

The creature looked down, repulsed by the sight of its own body. Its hands were the hands of a stranger, its fingers thick and clumsy. Its massive, bandaged arms hung down in grotesque proportion to its lean torso.

He wasn't human. He was a monster. And he belonged dead . . .

The thing in the cage looked helplessly at the two girls. They were watching him carefully, their eyes shining with hope.

The creature tried again. It pressed a gray finger against a string, and plucked. The string snapped, lashing out like a thin steel whip and striking the creature's face.

The thing in the cage roared.

Blinded by rage, it tilted back its head and unleashed a heart-wrenching cry. With strong, tensed fingers, it pounded and strummed the guitar. It clawed at the strings, growling and grunting with every savage chord—a demonic symphony of tortured sound.

Then, with a single piercing howl, it swung the guitar up and around and down . . .

And smashed it to pieces.

2

As the Hearse Goes By

From a popular children's rhyme known as "The Hearse Song."

Don't you ever laugh as the hearse goes by,
For you may be the next to die.
They wrap you up in a big white sheet
From your head down to your feet.
They put you in a big black box
And cover you up with dirt and rocks.
All goes well for about a week,
Then your coffin begins to leak.
The worms crawl in, the worms crawl out,
The worms play pinochle on your snout . . .

The sky over Thunder Lake High School was gray and bleak. A gentle mist washed over the building, and the red brick walls turned black in long glossy streaks—like tears.

Sara sat at her desk during homeroom period, star-

ing out the window as a thick blanket of clouds covered the town in a dreamy haze. She could barely
make out Josh's house on the other side of the lake.
The tall bedroom tower rose up in the fog like the
giant mast of a ghost ship . . .

To Sara, the mansion didn't look real.

It looked like something out of a nightmare.

Then a cold realization sunk in—*real life can be
worse than any nightmare.*

Sara stared at the house across the lake, remem-
bering how she used to call it "the haunted mansion." Well, now it was truly haunted—by the monster in the cage, the monster she created with her own
hands . . .

Josh . . .

Sara put her head down on the desk and closed her
eyes. She listened to the voice of her biology teacher,
Miss Nevils, reading the morning announcements: a
Pep Club meeting after school, yearbook staff meeting, football practice, band practice . . .

It all seemed so meaningless to Sara, as dreamy and
unreal as the mist outside the window.

Then Miss Nevils said something that made Sara
sit up and open her eyes.

"We'll all have a chance to pay our last respects to
Moose Morgan today," the teacher announced grimly. "The funeral procession will pass by the school
at nine o'clock, so we're asking all the students to
assemble on the sidewalk out front. If you wish to
attend, please exit the building in a quiet and order-
ly fashion immediately after the morning homeroom
bell."

Sara couldn't believe it—Moose Morgan's hearse driving past the school? She knew that today was his funeral, but she never expected anything like this.

Can I do it? Sara wondered. Can I stand there and watch his funeral procession go by?

She felt her heart sinking as she listened to Miss Nevils read the rest of the announcement.

"Attendance is not required, but strongly encouraged. We hope that you will show your full support of the Morgan family in their time of grief, and we ask that you all take a moment to reflect on the tragedy in your own special way. Thank you. Sincerely, Principal Frear."

The room was quiet for a moment—an unusual event during homeroom period. Sara swore she could hear her own heart pounding, louder and louder.

She was afraid her classmates would hear it, too.

Then the room was filled with whispers, and the whispers turned into chatter, and the chatter into noise. Everyone was talking about Moose Morgan and how he killed himself by jumping off the roof of the school. Everyone had a theory . . .

"Heather Leigh Clark broke his heart."

"No, he lost out on a football scholarship."

"I heard he was overdosing on steroids."

They passed their theories back and forth, from desk to desk, spicing it all with gossip and rumors and lies.

But Sara knew the truth.

Moose Morgan didn't jump.

He was thrown off the roof by the resurrected corpse

of Joshua Frank. And Sara was the one who brought the monster to life.

It's my fault, she thought. I'm the one who's responsible for Moose's death.

Her heart was pounding harder now. She felt like a character in an Edgar Allan Poe story—her telltale heart beating louder and louder, teasing her, tormenting her, forcing her to blurt out a tearful confession . . .

But then the school bell rang.

And Sara knew what she had to do.

She filed out of the classroom with the other students and pushed her way through the hall to her locker. She turned the combination lock, opened the door, and reached for her jacket.

It was time to pay her last respects to Moose Morgan.

The hallways were louder, more active than usual. There was a buzz in the air—everyone was going to watch the funeral procession.

In a daze, Sara walked slowly to the lobby of the school. Mobs of students crowded around the doors, pushing their way out onto the sidewalk. Sara shuffled ahead, her mind numb. She glanced down at the trophy case in the lobby—and saw Moose Morgan's football trophy.

Her eyes filled with tears.

She had to admit that she never liked Moose Morgan—and that Moose had probably attacked Josh on that fateful night—but he was still a human being. He didn't deserve to die.

The cold mist tickled Sara's face as she stepped through the front doors of the school. She moved through a crowd of students, her head turning from side to side, searching . . .

"Sara!"

It was Jessie. She was standing in a puddle, wearing a yellow raincoat with a hood, and she waved and splashed around in the water. She reminded Sara of a little duck, and somehow that made Sara feel a little better.

"Jessie!"

The two girls embraced. Jessie whispered in Sara's ear, "I'm glad you're here. I didn't think I could watch this alone."

Sara didn't say anything. Her eyes said it all. Jessie reached for her hand and squeezed it gently. "Is Eddie here?" Sara asked.

"I don't know," said Jessie, looking around. "It's so crowded. Everybody in the school is out here. I guess if you give them the choice between first-period class and a funeral, they'll pick the funeral."

"Most of these people never even knew Moose Morgan."

"The lucky ones."

"Jessie! Show some respect."

"Sorry."

Sara stood on her toes and craned her neck. Through the crowds of students, she saw a tall, thin boy with longish black hair and a baseball cap.

"Eddie! Over here!"

Eddie Perez turned his head. His dark eyes lit up when he saw Sara standing next to Jessie. He flashed a grim smile and walked along the sidewalk toward them. Sara noticed he had an air of confidence in the way he moved—a new posture and attitude that was so different from the nerdy way he used to be before . . .

Before he helped Sara and Jessie create a monster.

"Sara! Jessie! I thought I'd never find you in this mob!" He leaned forward and gave them each a quick peck on the cheek.

Sara was surprised. The old Eddie Perez would never have kissed a girl's cheek like that.

Eddie had changed—for the better—but Sara couldn't help thinking about the gruesome events that turned the shy, withdrawn boy into a man . . . He helped her steal body parts from the morgue. He wired up the computer and electrodes that brought Josh to life. And finally, he managed to confess his love for Sara.

"How are you holding up, Sara?" he whispered in her ear.

She looked into his warm, dark eyes and shrugged her shoulders. "I don't know," she said quietly. "I feel like a criminal visiting the scene of the crime."

Eddie nodded. "Me, too."

Tears welled up in Sara's eyes. "I feel so guilty," she said, her voice cracking.

The boy put his arm around her shoulders. "It's not our fault, Sara. We tried to stop it. But some things are out of our control."

She stared at Eddie through her tears, then threw her arms around his neck and hugged him. She felt so confused. In spite of everything, she still loved Josh. But how could she explain the way she felt about Eddie?

"Sara! Eddie! *Sweethearts!*"

They cringed when they heard the voice of Heather Leigh Clark. Sara and Eddie broke away from each other and turned to face the tall blond cheerleader. "Hello, Heather," Sara muttered.

Heather was wearing black from head to toe. Her dress was obviously expensive and embroidered with black lace and pearls. And she wore enough makeup to frost a cake.

"It's so tragic, isn't it?" Heather said, dabbing her dry eyes with a black silk handkerchief. "I still can't believe that Moose is dead. It was only a few days ago that he professed his love to me."

She blew her nose in the handkerchief. Sara rolled her eyes. "You must be devastated," she said.

Heather waved the handkerchief and sniffed. "*Totally* devastated," she answered. "But I'm trying to be philosophical about this. After all, love and death go hand in hand, don't they?"

Sara shivered, but didn't say anything.

How could she tell Heather the truth? Moose didn't kill himself for her. He was murdered . . .

"Moose must have loved me so much," Heather continued. "And that love ended in death." She glanced back and forth from Sara to Eddie. "I see that, even in this time of death, a new love has been born."

Eddie cleared his throat nervously.

"Eddie and I are just friends," Sara explained.

Heather batted her eyes. "What does your *boyfriend* Josh think about your . . . friendship?"

"Josh likes Eddie, too."

"And where *is* Josh?" Heather leered. "He still can't be sick. He hasn't been in school all year!"

Sara closed her eyes. "There have been some complications," she said.

Heather laughed and waved her handkerchief at Eddie. "How do you like that, Eddie?" she said. "Sara called you a *complication*."

Eddie smiled. "You ought to hear what she calls *you*," he said coldly. "Please, excuse us. We're here to pay our respects to the dead . . . not put on a fashion show."

He turned his back on the blond cheerleader. Heather glared, then spun around with her nose in the air. "What a thing to say to a girl who's in mourning!" She stormed away.

Sara looked up at Eddie in amazement. "Where'd you get the guts to talk back to Heather Leigh Clark?" she asked.

Eddie shrugged. "She deserved it."

"Well, you've probably ruined your chances to date any girl in the cheerleading squad."

Eddie looked into Sara's blue eyes. "I don't want to date any girl in the cheerleading squad, Sara," he said. "There's only one girl I want . . ."

His eyes burned with longing.

Sara's face turned red. She didn't know what to say. But Jessie came to the rescue.

"Look! Down the street! It's coming!"

A hush fell over the students in front of the school. Everyone stopped talking, stopped moving, and turned their heads toward the end of the street.

Out of the mist, a long black hearse rolled silently

over the glistening concrete—like the phantom carriage of Death itself. It glided through the fog, slow and unstoppable, a shining steel vessel of darkness. And resting inside, behind polished windows and white curtains, was the casket of Moose Morgan.

Sara trembled. As the hearse moved closer and closer, her heart pounded louder and faster.

Soon, it was floating in front of her, so close she could reach out and touch it. A horrible vision flashed through her mind—the corpse of Moose Morgan smashing through the casket, shattering the glass, and grabbing Sara by the throat.

But that didn't happen.

It wasn't Moose's corpse that grabbed Sara by the throat. It was her own guilt.

She reached for Eddie's and Jessie's hands, and held them. Behind her, a boy started to sing, "The worms crawl in, the worms crawl out." The other boys giggled and tried to join along. Sara spun around.

"Shut up! It's not funny!" she said.

The boys stifled their laughs, and Sara turned back to the funeral procession. The hearse moved on, and it was followed by a long black limousine. Moose's family sat in the backseat—his mother, his father, his brother . . .

A silent tear rolled down Sara's cheek.

They looked like such nice people. Moose's brother, Mike, was a freshman in Jessie's class. Jessie said Mike was a cool kid, nothing like his older brother.

The pain in Sara's heart intensified as she studied Mike's face through the window of the passing car.

He was cute, with a pug nose and dirty blond hair. His face was warm and open, but shadowed by sadness and grief.

Then, as Sara watched the limousine go by, something strange happened . . .

Mike Morgan turned his head, his blue eyes fixed on Jessie. Then he smiled. And winked at her.

Jessie winked back and waved.

And the long black car moved on, followed by more cars filled with relatives and friends.

Sara looked over at Jessie. "What was that all about?" she asked.

"What?" said Jessie, playing innocent.

"Mike Morgan winked at you," said Sara. "And you winked back."

Jessie shifted back and forth, hiding her eyes under the yellow hood of her raincoat. "I was afraid to tell you," she said quietly.

"Tell me what?"

Jessie closed her eyes and sighed. "Mike asked me out on a date."

Sara's jaw dropped. "Moose Morgan's brother?" she said. "Asked you out on a date?"

"Weird, huh?" said Jessie, staring down at the wet sidewalk.

"What did you tell him?"

"I told him I have to ask my grandfather."

"What are you going to do?"

Jessie sighed. "I don't know," she whispered. "I feel funny about it. After all, my brother killed his brother."

Sara bit her lip and watched the funeral procession

disappear into the fog. The mist blurred her vision. And the words of Heather Leigh Clark echoed in her brain . . .

Love and death go hand in hand, don't they?

3

The Kiss of Death

From the diary of Sara Watkins . . .

The human heart is the strongest and toughest organ in the body. Why then does it seem so fragile?

When I resurrected Josh from the dead, I promised to love and care for him forever. But when I looked into those lifeless eyes—and imagined kissing those ravaged lips—I wondered how strong my love really was. Did I only love him for his beautiful face, his body, his voice? Or did I love the soul within? My heart couldn't answer these questions—but it wouldn't let me abandon Josh, either.

So my heart remained divided. And a heart divided will surely fall.

The green mountains of Thunder Lake seemed to change overnight. The leaves in the trees turned golden orange, and the morning sun intensified its rays to highlight the colors of autumn. It was a beautiful sight to behold. But beneath the breathtaking veil of gold and red and orange, there was the dark cold specter of winter . . .

One by one, the leaves twisted and turned in the wind. And one by one, they fell—leaving a skeleton of bare branches, a graveyard of naked trees.

Sara and Eddie brushed the leaves out of their hair as they walked up the path to the Frank family mansion. Before they reached the door, Eddie stopped and looked around.

"What is it?" Sara asked.

Eddie smiled and raised his arms. "All this," he said, waving at the mountains and trees. "It's so beautiful. I love autumn. It makes me think of pumpkin pie."

Sara sighed. "It makes me think of death," she said, knocking on the front door of the mansion.

Eddie dropped his arms to his sides, feeling a little stupid. "There's nothing wrong with appreciating beauty," he said. "Even if there's death in the world."

Sara leaned against the door and looked into Eddie's eyes. "I know," she said. "You're right, Eddie." She opened her mouth to say something else—but the door swung open and Sara tumbled inside.

"Sara!"

Grandfather Frank tried to catch her in his arms, but his gnarled hands were weak. She slipped through his grasp and fell to the floor.

"Oh, dear, I'm sorry," the old man said, trying to help her up. "These blasted hands of mine . . . Not only have they ruined my career as a surgeon, they've made it impossible for me to rescue a young damsel in distress."

Eddie jumped in to help Sara to her feet. But he couldn't help staring at Grandfather Frank's hands—they were thin, twisted, and covered with old scars.

"What happened to your hands?" Eddie asked.

Sara flashed an angry glance at Eddie. She had always wanted to know what happened to Grandfather Frank's hands—but she thought it was rude to ask.

The old man smiled at Eddie. "That's a long story, my boy," he said. "Someday, perhaps, I'll tell you."

Sara felt embarrassed. So she changed the subject. "How's Josh today?" she asked.

Grandfather Frank hid his hands behind his back. "I really don't know," he said. "I don't go into the cellar very often. My presence seems to upset him."

Sara frowned. "That's odd," she said. "Josh loves you, Professor Frank. I know he does."

The old man shrugged his narrow shoulders. "I don't take it personally," he said. "Josh strangled his own dog, after all."

Sara shivered. As long as she lived, she would never forget that horrible night. She could still see Josh's monstrous hands wrapped around Baskerville's throat, squeezing tighter and tighter, until the struggling dog fell limp to the floor. The vision was burned in her brain forever . . .

She took a deep breath and turned to Eddie. "I want you to go the old mill later on and run those tests on Baskerville. He might look like a normal dog, but who knows what effects the reanimation may have had on him. Maybe we can learn what went wrong with Josh."

"Sure," said Eddie. "I'll check up on Frankendog."

"Frankendog?" Sara rolled her eyes. "Let's go see Josh before I die laughing." She grabbed Eddie by the arm and pulled him across the entry hall.

"Good luck," said Grandfather Frank.

The two teenagers walked to the door under the stairs. Eddie opened it for Sara, tilted his head, and said, "After you." Sara grasped the old wooden railing. She flicked the light switch and walked carefully, step by step, into the cellar.

"It smells down here," said Eddie, making a face.

Sara didn't say anything. She walked through the first basement room and unlocked the heavy oak door to the second room. She could hear something moving inside . . .

He was waiting for her.

Her heart was racing. Adrenaline surged through her body, heightening the fear and dread that gripped her every time she saw him.

Josh . . .

He was sitting in the far corner of the cage. His head was slumped forward, his black matted hair hanging over his face. His arms were folded across his chest, which rose and fell in long, deep breaths. On the floor, by his side, were the splintered remains of the broken guitar.

He used to play love songs on that guitar, Sara thought bitterly. Love songs that he wrote just for me.

In the shadows of her mind, she heard the haunting strains of Josh's music—the eerie chords of his guitar, the tender longing in his voice, the dark poetry of his lyrics . . .

It's the heart that beats forever . . . the love that never dies . . .

He wrote those words for me, Sara thought. And he wrote them only days before he killed himself.

The memory of Josh's music faded away as she studied the thing in the cage. The only sound she heard now was the creature's breathing—a low unearthly growl that ebbed and flowed from his throat.

"Is he asleep?" Eddie whispered.

"Shhh."

Sara stood still as she watched the bandaged monstrosity slowly lift its head. The hair fell away from its hideously scarred face. And its eyes—so green and so cold—seemed to look right through her.

"Sa . . . ra."

The horrible sound of his voice made her blood run cold. It wasn't a human voice at all. It was the voice of a dead thing.

She swallowed and tried to smile. "Hello, Josh," she said. "Won't you say hello to me?"

The creature parted its black lips. A yellow stream of saliva dripped down its chin.

"Sa . . . ra."

Sara nodded. "Sara, that's me," she said. "That's very good, Josh. You know my name. Sara."

The creature grunted and exposed its dull white teeth. The gray flesh pulled tighter across its rigid cheekbones, and its lips cracked and split as the scarred face twisted into a gruesome expression . . .

He was trying to smile.

But it wasn't really a smile at all. It looked more like a snarl, a sneer, a grotesque mockery of a smile.

Sara started to cry.

She couldn't help it. The tears were burning her cheeks, melting away the strength she had tried so hard to summon up in her soul.

Why? she thought to herself. Why did you kill yourself, Josh? Why did I bring you back to life? Why is all this happening? Why . . . ?

She fell into Eddie's arms, sobbing.

He held her tight and pressed his lips against her ear. "It's okay," he whispered. "It's okay to cry."

Sara leaned into Eddie and gasped for air. "But I . . . I have to be strong . . ."

With gentle fingers, he stroked her hair. "You don't have to be strong all the time, Sara."

She closed her eyes and swallowed. "Sometimes . . . I just can't look at him . . . His eyes . . . His eyes make me feel so guilty. How can I love him when I can't even look at him?"

"It's okay," Eddie whispered.

"It's not okay," Sara sobbed. "I've turned him into a monster, Eddie. He killed his own dog. And he killed Moose Morgan. Yesterday, when I saw Moose's family in the funeral procession, I wanted to scream and confess everything. I wanted to be punished . . . because I'm selfish, I'm evil . . ."

"You're wonderful, Sara," said Eddie. "You risked everything for the boy you loved. You wanted him to live again."

"But I can't even look at him . . . I'm terrified of him."

Eddie pressed his lips against her neck. "But you still love him, Sara. I know you do."

She looked up into Eddie's eyes. She could feel his chest pressed against her, his heart pounding, almost bursting, with emotion. She knew that Eddie loved her—and respected her feelings for Josh. But now, Sara wasn't sure if those feelings were still alive . . .

Like Josh, her love was neither dead nor alive. It was an unnatural thing—artificial, resurrected, and held together with bandages and clamps.

"If I love Josh," she whispered to Eddie, "then why do I fear him?"

Eddie tilted his head. "There's nothing wrong with being afraid."

"But I don't want to be afraid," she said, closing her eyes. "I want to be strong and rational. I'm the promising young scientist, remember?"

"You're also a woman, Sara," Eddie said in a low, deep voice. "With a human heart and a soul."

A single tear fell down her face. She looked up at Eddie, at his dark wavy hair, his warm eyes, his soft lips . . .

She wanted to kiss him.

The urge was so powerful, she could hardly resist. Here with Eddie, hidden away from the rest of the world, Sara was no longer the school science whiz with a heart of stone. She was a young woman with human desires. And this tall dark boy was no longer Eduardo Perez, Thunder Lake's one and only Puerto Rican computer nerd. He was Eddie, the one and only boy Sara could open her heart to . . .

She tilted her head and leaned forward. Their lips met, soft and warm at first, then harder and more insistent. She wrapped her arms around Eddie's back and pulled him closer, feeling the strength flow from his body into hers. They leaned against the bars of the cage. They hugged, they kissed . . .

And the horrors of life and death disappeared. The pain, the guilt, the terror—they all faded away like a bad dream.

For the first time since Josh's suicide, Sara felt safe, and warm, and happy . . .

Until the creature grabbed Eddie by the throat.

It happened so fast, Sara could barely catch her breath.

One moment, she was kissing Eddie, her mind light-years away from reality. The next moment, she and Eddie were torn apart in a sudden burst of violence . . .

Reality had returned with a vengeance.

And that vengeance was a raging, howling thing that used to be her boyfriend.

I'm sorry, Josh . . .

The thought echoed in her mind as Eddie was wrenched away from her, his arms thrashing against the bars. She watched in horror as the creature locked its powerful hands around the boy's neck and squeezed. Sara was frozen with fear, her heart paralyzed with shame. But somehow, she managed to scream.

"Josh! No!"

The thing in the cage was furious. It roared and tightened its grip around Eddie's throat, and slammed the boy's head against the bars. A howl of pain was choked off by the monster's fingers.

Sara shrieked.

"Josh! Listen to me! Josh! No!"

The creature snarled and howled in rage. It pulled Eddie up against the bars and grasped his throat even tighter.

Eddie struggled in the monster's grip, but couldn't reach around to pry himself loose. He could barely breathe. His face turned white as he felt himself blacking out.

"No, Josh!"

Sara lunged at Josh's wrists, grasping the flesh near the stitches and pulling as hard as she could.

"Stop it, Josh! It's me! Sara! Sara!"

The thing in the cage stopped howling. Its icy green eyes focused on Sara's face. Its contorted face softened and its lips parted . . .

"Sa . . . ra."

"Yes! It's Sara, Josh! Let him go, Josh. Sara says let him go."

For a short fleeting moment, Sara thought she saw a flash of recognition in the creature's cold, dead eyes. Recognition, and something else. Warmth. Love . . .

"Sara says let him go, Josh."

The monstrous fingers loosened around Eddie's neck.

"That's it, Josh. Let him go."

Slowly, the creature released the boy. Eddie fell to the floor, coughing and gasping for breath. Then a strange, unearthly hush fell over the room.

Sara's first impulse was to help Eddie. But she couldn't move, or breathe, or even blink her eyes. She was held spellbound by the thing in the cage. He looked . . . different . . . somehow.

"Josh?"

Holding her breath, she took a step forward and peered through the bars. The creature quickly covered his face with his hands.

"Look at me, Josh."

Slowly, with trembling hands, the thing in the cage exposed his face to Sara. And when she saw what his hands were hiding, it broke her heart into a million pieces . . .

He was hiding the tears in his eyes.

"Oh, Josh . . ."

The expression on his face was the saddest, most soulful thing Sara had ever seen. It was filled with heartache, and love, and longing . . .

It was the face of the boy she loved.

Her eyes filled with tears as he raised his bandaged arm and reached through the bars of the cage.

"*Sa . . . ra.*"

His hand was open, his fingers trembling with fear and loneliness.

Sara whispered his name. "Josh . . ."

And she reached out to take his hand into her own.

When their fingers touched, a heart-wrenching sigh escaped Josh's lips. A tear fell across his cheek. And gently, he closed his hand over the Frank family ring on her finger.

Sara smiled through her tears.

"I love you, Josh."

She stared into his eyes and squeezed his hand. Then, she moved closer and closer until her face was pressed against the bars.

Josh leaned forward, and Sara felt her lips brush against the ravaged flesh of his face, his cheek, his lips . . .

And she kissed the thing in the cage.

On the floor by her feet, Eddie watched in silence. The girl who had kissed him—only moments ago— was reaching into the creature's cage, stroking its face and whispering in its ear . . .

"I'll love you forever."

4

Everyday Tortures

From a song written by Joshua Frank six months before he killed himself . . .

She cuts with her words,
*   He stabs with his eyes.*
She slices, he dices,
*   They injure with lies.*
The pain that we give
*   Is the pain that we take.*
And the hurt that we hide
*   Is the hurt that we make.*

We're everyday victims, just trying to heal
*   The everyday tortures we try not to feel . . .*

When Joshua Frank performed "Everyday Tortures" at the Junior Prom last year, very few people understood the song's dark, bitter message. And yet Josh's portrayal of daily abuse applied to anyone who felt pain—and everyone who inflicted it. In fact, the song could apply to a typical day at Thunder Lake High School . . .

9:15 A.M. **The Computer Room.**

Eddie Perez sat at the terminal, working on a program that could process a series of medical charts and graphs. He was doing it for Sara.

Lately, he was doing a lot of things for Sara.

Because he loved her. He couldn't help it.

Pushing the long black hair out of his eyes, Eddie sighed and stared at the monitor. A medical chart flashed on the screen in color-coded graphics. When the program was finished, the computer would supply a complete evaluation on the health and fitness of Josh's reanimated dog, Baskerville. It was a lot of work, but Eddie had promised Sara he'd do it.

If the truth be known, he'd promise her anything. Even if she still loved Josh.

I'll love you forever . . .

Sara's words echoed in Eddie's mind. Deep down, he wished she had spoken those words to him—not the thing in the cage. But Eddie knew that Josh meant everything to Sara. And why not? Josh was the kind of boy Eddie had always envied. He wore the right clothes and hung out with the right people. But he wasn't a snob—everybody liked him. Everything about him was cool. Eddie had even grown his hair out longer to be a little more like Josh.

But Josh had something else—the soul of an artist

that shined through his music—and Eddie could never compete with that.

Or could he?

Eddie scratched his head and looked around the computer room. Four other students were busy at their keyboards. The door was wide open, but the hallway was empty.

Maybe I can write her a poem, Eddie thought.

He cleared the screen of his computer and typed in the words "For Sara." Then he sat back in the chair and stared out the window at Thunder Lake. He closed his eyes, then opened them again. And he started to write . . .

Love is like a window.

He stopped and frowned. Love is like a window? he wondered. Then he typed the next line . . .

It opens and shuts.

Brilliant, he thought, rolling his eyes.

You can see right through it.

No kidding, he smirked.

Can you see my aching guts?

Eddie stared at the screen, reading his words—and laughing out loud. He couldn't control himself. His poem was so bad, it was hilarious.

"What's so funny, geek-face?"

Eddie looked up from his terminal to see two football jocks leaning in the doorway of the computer room. Jimbo and Crusher were two of Moose Morgan's best friends. And they were every bit as obnoxious as the late great quarterback.

"Let's see what's so funny," said Crusher, walking into the room and leaning over Eddie's shoulder.

"Hey, Jimbo, look! He wrote a love poem . . . for Sara!"

Jimbo staggered up behind Eddie. "Aw, how sweet."

Crusher put his arm around Eddie's neck. "So you're in love with Sara Watkins, huh? The Ice Witch? Well, I guess nerds really go for that egghead type."

"She's already got a boyfriend, idiot," said Jimbo, swatting Eddie's head.

"Yeah, but Josh has been real sick, hasn't he?" said Crusher. "So now's your chance. You gotta move fast. Ask her to the big Halloween Dance! You already got your nerd costume!"

Jimbo laughed at Crusher's joke and slapped him on the back. Eddie didn't say anything. He tensed up and prayed they'd leave him alone. Finally, the two boys turned to go. Eddie breathed a sigh of relief . . .

But Crusher stopped at the door. He shot a nasty grin at Jimbo, then turned and walked back to Eddie's terminal. The brawny boy leaned forward. He whispered in Eddie's ear . . .

"Love is like a window, Eddie. I can see your aching guts."

Then he punched Eddie in the stomach and left.

10:45 A.M. The Biology Room.

"You wanted to talk to me, Miss Nevils?"

"Yes, Sara, please have a seat."

Sara sat down in the front row of the empty classroom. Miss Nevils pushed her hair behind her ears

and removed her glasses. Then she leaned forward
and cleared her throat.

"I'm deeply disappointed in you, Sara."

Sara felt her stomach tie itself into a knot. She had
been waiting for something like this.

"I just finished grading yesterday's test. Bad news.
You're getting a C. Normally, I would think it was
just a fluke. But it's the third C you've gotten this
year."

Sara looked down at the desk and sighed.

"Then I went and talked to your other teachers,"
Miss Nevils continued. "Everyone is surprised at your
poor academic performance this year. You've ruined
a perfect straight A record. You've destroyed your
chance at becoming valedictorian."

Sara didn't take her eyes off the desk. She focused
on the scrawled words of graffiti: A MIND IS A TER-
RIBLE THING TO LOSE.

Miss Nevils leaned back in her chair. "What's
wrong, Sara?" she asked. "Why the sudden change?
You were my best student. You had a perfect record.
Now you stare out the window and never hand in your
assignments on time. You seem like you're a million
miles away."

Sara looked up and glared at Miss Nevils. "It's
personal," she said. "I told you that already."

The teacher sighed. "Yes, I remember," she said.
"And that's why I did what I did."

Sara frowned. "What did you do?"

Miss Nevils cleared her throat again. "I had no
other choice. None of the teachers can get through
to you, Sara."

"What did you do?" Sara demanded.

The teacher shifted in her seat and told her . . .

"I've sent a letter to your parents."

12:20 P.M. The Music Room.

"Come on, Jessie, before someone sees us."

Mike Morgan dragged Jessie by the arm into the music room. She glanced around at the empty seats and music stands. Mike's tuba was propped up in the corner.

"We're gonna get caught," said Jessie.

"No way!" said Mike with a grin. "Everyone's eating lunch now. Relax. I just want to talk to you."

"Why couldn't you talk to me in the cafeteria?"

" 'Cause I'm shy and sensitive."

"Yeah, right. Just like me," said Jessie, looking around the room. "Is that your tuba?"

"Ain't she a beauty?" Mike pulled her across the room and pushed her into a chair. Then he hoisted the tuba over his head and onto his shoulder. "Listen."

Jessie smirked as Mike Morgan puffed out his cheeks and blew into the mouthpiece. A long, low note blasted from the tuba. Then he started playing "Stairway to Heaven."

Jessie laughed and clapped her hands. "I never heard Led Zeppelin played on a tuba before."

Mike grinned. "That's 'cause you ain't hanging out with the right people. Stick with me, kid, and we'll make beautiful music together."

Jessie smiled.

She liked Mike. He was funny and cute—with his little pug nose and goofy grin. He was always cheerful, always clowning around . . .

Even two days after his brother's funeral.

Jessie's smile disappeared.

The memory of her brother, Josh, throwing Moose Morgan off the roof of the school still haunted her, still gave her nightmares.

Mike noticed the look on Jessie's face. "What's wrong?" he asked.

Jessie shrugged. "I was just thinking about your brother," she said. "It must be awful . . . to lose your own brother like that."

She couldn't tell him that her own brother threw himself from the tower and killed himself.

"You must be all broken up about it," she whispered.

Mike sighed. He lifted the tuba over his head and rested it on its stand. Then he moved closer to Jessie.

"It's strange," he said. "My parents don't think I should be here at school. They think I should be at home, grieving. But they don't understand. I *am* grieving . . . in my own way. I laugh and make jokes 'cause if I didn't, I'd burst out crying, you know?"

Jessie nodded. "I know . . . I'm the same way."

Mike leaned back in his chair. "We're just a couple of flakes," he said. "At least, that's what my parents think I am. They don't understand why I don't wanna play football, like Moose. They're always nagging me to give up the tuba and join the team. They say marching band is for sissies, can you believe that? My own parents! Even my mom!"

"What do you tell them?"

Mike smirked. "I tell 'em so what, I'm a big sissy! The biggest sissy of all! And I'm fighting for sissy rights everywhere!"

Jessie burst out laughing. "You're a scream, Mike."

"Yeah, I know," he said. "That's why I'm asking you to the Halloween Dance. 'Cause two screams are better than one."

Jessie smiled on the outside—but inside, she was a total mess. How could she date Mike Morgan? Her brother had killed Moose with his bare hands! It just wasn't right. It was crazy, it was weird, it was demented . . .

And it was exactly what Jessie wanted to do.

"Okay, I'll go with you," she said. "As long as you don't make me wear some stupid Halloween costume."

Mike grinned. "I promise I won't make you wear a stupid Halloween costume," he said, pausing and smiling. "I'll make you wear a *brilliant* Halloween costume!"

Jessie groaned.

And Mike moved closer and closer. He was no longer smiling now. The look on his face was dead serious.

"I like you, Jessie," he whispered. "A lot."

Then he brought his face closer to Jessie's—as if he were about to kiss her.

Jessie panicked. She didn't want to hurt Mike's feelings. She liked him more than any boy she had ever met. But for some reason, she wasn't ready to kiss him yet . . .

She was afraid.

"Jessie." Mike's voice was low and husky, his lips starting to pucker.

"Mike . . . no . . ."

She started to protest, but it was too late. Mike forced his lips hard against hers. His hands gripped her shoulders. She closed her eyes and tried to enjoy the sensation. But her mind was spinning with emotions—guilt, fear, passion, grief . . .

And when she opened her eyes to look at Mike's face, all she could see was a smaller version of Moose Morgan . . .

The boy her brother killed.

2:35 P.M. The Library.

"Please, Sara, please! You've *got* to help me!"

Sara stared at Heather Leigh Clark with a look of total disbelief. After all, the head cheerleader was throwing herself at Sara's feet, begging and pleading . . .

"I don't have *time* to be on the Decorating Committee! I thought I was volunteering to decorate the *Prom*, not the *Halloween Dance*! I simply *can't* do it!"

Sara rolled her eyes. "What makes you think *I* have the time to decorate the Halloween Dance, Heather?"

Heather shrugged. "I dunno. I figured, since Josh is sick, you might have more time on your hands. Anyway, you're so smart and everything, I bet you could whip up some *killer* decorations."

Sara looked down at her biology book. "I'm too busy," she said. "And why should I help you out? All you do is say nasty things about me and my friends. You spread lies and rumors about me and Eddie Perez . . ."

"Sara! Darling!" Heather gushed. "I was kidding! Gosh, can't you take a joke! Anyway, I'll make it up to you. I promise I'll set the record straight about you and Eddie. You two are just friends, right?"

"Right," Sara muttered.

"Will you do it, Sara? Please?" Heather begged. "Will you *please* decorate the Halloween Dance for me?"

Sara closed her eyes and thought about it.

There were so many things on her mind—so many mixed feelings about Josh . . . and Eddie . . . and herself . . .

"Okay, Heather," she said. "I'll do it."

The cheerleader jumped up and down. "Excellent!"

"But first," Sara interrupted, "I'd like to ask a small favor."

3:30 P.M. The Hallway.

"You're asking *me*? To the Halloween Dance?"

Eddie couldn't believe his ears. Here he was, standing in the hall by his locker, talking to Kiki Austin, one of the prettiest cheerleaders in the school . . .

And she was asking him out on a date.

"Sure, Eddie," she said, cracking her gum. "The dance starts at eight o'clock. So how about you pick me up at nine."

"Are you sure?" Eddie asked, staring at the gorgeous redhead.

"Sure, I'm sure," said Kiki. "If we go at nine o'clock, we won't be the first ones there. Here's my address."

She handed him a pink slip of paper. Eddie took it and blinked his eyes. "But . . . Kiki . . ."

"Just don't wear a costume that looks too silly," she said under her breath. "I'm gonna dress up as a fairy princess, so try to wear something, you know, appropriate. See you next week!"

Then she turned and disappeared into a crowd of students.

Eddie was in shock.

He lurched down the hall, like a zombie, clutching the pink slip of paper in his hand. Finally, he saw Sara at her locker. "Sara."

She turned. "Hi, Eddie," she said. "What's wrong? You look like you saw a ghost."

"No. Ghosts don't ask boys out on dates," he said in a daze.

"What are you talking about?"

Eddie leaned forward and whispered. "Kiki Austin just asked me to take her to the Halloween Dance."

Sara smiled. "That's great, Eddie. She's a very pretty girl."

Eddie shook his head. "It doesn't make any sense," he said. "She's a cheerleader. She belongs to that Heather Leigh Clark crowd. Why on earth would she ask me out?"

Sara shrugged her shoulders. "I don't know. Because you're cute?"

"I'm not cute."

"Yes, you are, Eddie. Especially since you grew your hair longer."

So I could look more like Josh, he thought with a twinge of pain.

Sara put her hand on his arm. "Look, Eddie," she said. "I think it's great that a girl asked you out. You're cute, you're funny, you're smart. Why should you waste all your time with me?" She lowered her voice. "Look, I'm sorry about everything that's happened. I love you, Eddie, as a friend. But I love Josh, too. It's not fair to you. So I think you should go on this date and have some fun."

Eddie sighed and looked down at the floor. He could feel the tears building in his eyes. But he refused to let Sara see him cry . . .

"Okay, I'll go," he said. "But there's one thing that bothers me. What if Heather and her gang are just setting me up for a cruel joke? I don't want to end up at the dance with a bucket of blood dumped on my head."

Sara laughed. "Don't be paranoid," she said. "Just relax and go to the dance. I want you to have fun."

Eddie sulked. "Is there anything else you want me to do?"

Sara squinted her eyes. "Well . . . I hate to ask, but would you mind going to the mill tonight and trying out your new medical program on Baskerville?"

Eddie smiled bitterly.

"Sure," he said. "Anything you want, Sara."

Then he turned and walked away.

"See you, Eddie," Sara whispered as she watched

him disappear into a crowd of students.

Suddenly, she felt an overwhelming sadness. She wished she had never asked Heather to find a date for Eddie. And she wished she could explain why she felt so empty and alone . . .

It was almost as if her heart were breaking.

5

Lightning Strikes Again

Like Josh's broken body after the fall, my heart was shattered into a million pieces. But unlike Josh, the damage could not be repaired with needle and thread.

How could I stitch up my sadness? My confusion? My life?

My heart was a dead thing, waiting to be struck by lightning. Not by a bolt of madness and rage that created a monster—but of inspiration and truth that could set me free.

Once again, I got what I wished for. And once again, it was not what I expected.

The storm descended upon Thunder Lake like a predator closing in on its prey.

With cold, silent precision, the clouds stalked the town from a distance, circling the lake behind a veil of mountains, then gliding stealthily over the treetops. Soon the town was covered by darkness. The storm held its position. It watched. It waited. It gathered up the untapped power of its rain, its thunder, its lightning . . .

And then it pounced.

The thing in the cage felt it first—long before any man, woman, or child in Thunder Lake even realized it was raining.

Down in the basement, locked behind bars, the creature heard the low rumble of thunder. And he knew there was lightning in the air, even though he couldn't see its blinding flash.

He *felt* the lightning.

Sharp, tingling waves of power coursed through the blue artificial blood in his veins. Electrical energy pulsed and surged through every steel part in his body—the clamps that fastened his arms and legs to his torso . . . the wires that connected the nerves in his joints . . . the electrodes that pierced his neck and penetrated his spinal cord . . .

His whole body was *alive* with lightning.

It made him feel good. And strong.

The creature had never known such strength. Ever since the night Sara brought him to life, he felt nothing but misery and pain. His body was a stranger. The heart that pounded in his chest was not his own—it was an alien thing, like the organs that wriggled in his guts with a life of their own.

He hated his body, and his heart, and his face . . .

How could Sara ever love something so ugly and horrible?

He watched her sitting in the corner of the room next to the little music box. Sara had fallen asleep, her hair falling down over her face. But the music kept playing . . .

> *"Time, it makes the prison.*
> *Fate, it holds the key.*
> *Death, it takes the prisoner,*
> *But love will set us free."*

The creature listened to the strange voice and knew that it was his own—before he died. And in his alien heart, he knew he would never be able to sing like that again . . .

"Forever and ever and ever . . . your love can keep me alive . . . forever and ever and ever . . ."

Tears welled up in the creature's glowing green eyes as he listened to the last verse .

> *"No matter where my soul rests,*
> *or where my body lies,*
> *It's the heart that beats forever,*
> *the love that never dies."*

In the corner, Sara shifted and groaned in her sleep. The creature watched her, longingly, and wondered if she was having a nightmare.

Then a loud thunderclap shook the house. An invisible wave of electricity surged through the creature. And the strength and rage that pulsed through his bandaged body made him realize that Sara would never sleep well again . . .

Because he was her nightmare.

The dream seemed so real to Sara.

Everything was the same at it was on the night they resurrected Josh. The old mill was transformed into a laboratory with bubbling beakers and buzzing transformers. The sky was infused with thunder and lightning and rain. Sara stood over the lab table with rubber gloves and a scalpel, and Eddie and Jessie were helping her with the operation. It was just like that fateful night.

But something was different.

It wasn't Josh's body on the lab table.

It was a human heart. And it was shattered into a million pieces.

"Forceps," said Sara, holding out her hand.

Jessie handed her the forceps, and Sara tried to clamp the broken heart together.

"Needle and thread," she said.

Eddie handed her the needle and thread.

She held the organ in her fingers and tried to sew up the pieces, one by one. But the thread kept tearing, the heart falling apart in her hands.

"Try this," said Eddie, holding up a strange, heart-shaped instrument. "I made it . . . for you."

"No, try this," said the other assistant in a deep voice.

Suddenly Sara realized that her other assistant wasn't Jessie . . .

It was Josh.

And he was holding up the Frank family ring he

had given her on the night he killed himself.

Sara didn't know what to do. Should she take the heart-shaped thing from Eddie? Or the gold ring from Josh?

She looked down at the broken heart on the table and wondered who it belonged to. Then she glanced down at her bloodstained lab coat . . .

There was a hole in her chest.

The broken heart on the table was her own.

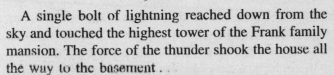

A single bolt of lightning reached down from the sky and touched the highest tower of the Frank family mansion. The force of the thunder shook the house all the way to the basement . . .

And Sara woke up with a jolt.

She rubbed her eyes and looked inside the cage. Josh was standing in the middle, his arms upraised, his muscles pulsating with a strange, invisible force.

"Josh?"

She stood up slowly and walked toward the cage. The sound of thunder vibrated the room, and the creature quivered in shock.

"Josh? Are you okay? Josh!"

Slowly he dropped his long arms to his sides and lowered his head. Through the black tangle of hair, his eyes were burning, glowing, with life.

Those eyes . . .

Sara had to turn away quickly. His eyes were so bright and forceful, they frightened her.

What's going on? she wondered.

Then he parted his lips and spoke . . .

"*Sa . . . ra.*"

His voice was like a cannon blast—a low, booming roar that echoed throughout the house.

It's the storm, Sara told herself. The lightning gives him strength.

Then she heard something else that chilled her to the bone . . .

An animal howled.

The unearthly, deafening sound rose up across the lake. The horrible baying of a hound . . .

It was Baskerville.

Sara recognized the dog's howl, amplified to an impossible volume. He was with Eddie in the old mill across the lake—but even from that distance, Sara could hear him clearly in the basement.

The lightning affects him, too, Sara thought with a shudder. That's all we need, reenergized monsters.

She looked up at Josh, standing in the center of the cage. His eyes were wide open, his hands clenched into fists. She had never seen him so tense. It scared her.

I have to get out of here, she thought.

She locked and bolted the room and climbed the cellar stairs as fast as she could. Then she stepped into the dark entry hall of the mansion.

Even with the sound and fury of the storm, the house seemed as silent and black as a tomb. Only the occasional flashes of lightning illuminated the shadows. Sara walked to the center of the entry hall and looked around.

No sign of life.

She was overwhelmed with a sudden desire to be

hugged and held and comforted. But no one could help her now. Grandfather Frank had retired to his study. Jessie was doing homework. Eddie was at the old mill with Baskerville.

And Sara had never felt so alone.

Josh . . .

She walked to the foot of the grand staircase and looked up. The gray wooden steps disappeared into darkness. Without thinking, she climbed the stairs, drifting like a ghost past each floor, moving higher and higher . . .

To Josh's bedroom in the tower.

She paused in the hallway outside his door. And she remembered how she used to stand there, listening to Josh play his music, before she'd burst through the door and cover his face with kisses . . .

Josh . . .

Even now, Sara could almost hear him on the other side of the door. But it didn't sound like singing.

Sara's heart skipped a beat.

Because someone was crying in Josh's room.

She held her breath and listened. And sure enough, she heard the sound of someone weeping on the other side of the door. A chill ran up her spine. Her hand was shaking as she reached for the doorknob and slowly pushed open the door . . .

"Jessie!" Sara gasped.

Josh's sister was sprawled across the bed, her face pressed against a pillow. And beside her, on the bed, was an open notebook.

Jessie looked up at Sara with bloodshot eyes. "Sara," she sobbed. "I think I'm going to kill myself."

Sara rushed to the bed and threw her arms around Josh's little sister. "Jessie?" she whispered. "What's wrong?"

The dark-haired girl choked on her tears. Finally, she managed to speak. "I heard the lightning hit the tower," she said. "So I came up to make sure nothing was damaged. When I got up here, I saw that the bookshelf had fallen. And I found that notebook on the floor . . ."

Sara glanced down at the open notebook and recognized Josh's printing. "What is it?"

Jessie closed her eyes. "It's sort of like a diary."

Sara felt something cold rush through her body. At first, she thought it was the storm and the wind. She turned and stared at the tower window of Josh's bedroom.

Why, Josh, why did you jump from that window?

It was bolted shut.

Another chill surged through Sara, caressing her face, her eyelashes, her lips . . .

Like a lover.

Or death itself.

She looked down at Jessie, weeping into the pillow. She had never seen her so upset. "Tell me, Jessie," Sara whispered. "Tell me everything."

Jessie took a deep breath, then pounded her fist on the bed. She gasped for air as she tried to speak through her tears. "The notebook . . . it . . . it . . ."

"What, Jessie?"

Sara held her breath, waiting for an answer. Deep in her heart, she knew it was something terrible.

Suddenly Jessie bolted up, her eyes dark and wild.

"Now I know why Josh killed himself!" she sobbed. "I know what it means to be a Frankenstein! And I know why I should probably kill myself, too!"

She flung herself down on the pillow, her body shaking violently. Sara threw her arms around her and held tight. She whispered in Jessie's ear.

"Don't say that, Jessie. Don't even think about killing yourself. I already lost my boyfriend . . . I don't think I could stand losing my best friend, too."

Jessie was breathing heavily, the tears flowing down her face. "You don't understand, Sara. Josh and I *have* to die. We shouldn't even be alive!"

"Stop saying that, Jessie!"

"It's the truth! It's sick and it's horrible, but it's the truth!"

Sara's mind was racing. She couldn't imagine what Jessie was talking about. What truth was so sick and horrible that Jessie would want to kill herself?

She whispered Jessie's name.

And Jessie sat up in the bed, her face flushed and streaked with tears, her eyes dull and cold. "Sara . . ." She tried to speak, but her eyes were fixed on the tower window.

Sara was frightened by the look on Jessie's face.

But she was even more frightened by the words that fell from Jessie's lips . . .

"Josh and I are the children of monsters."

The rain embraced the mansion tower like a mother with a crying child. Her voice was a soothing lullaby. Her arms hugged the gray tower walls, and her fingers stroked the rooftop gently, lovingly . . .

But the rain brought no comfort to Sara Watkins.

Because Jessie's words had struck her like a thunder-clap, more powerful than Mother Nature's storm.

Josh and I are the children of monsters.

Sara repeated the words over and over in her mind. But she couldn't quite grasp the meaning of them. If the words meant what Sara thought they meant, it was too horrible to comprehend.

Jessie saw the confusion on her face and tried to explain. "You know my parents died when I was a baby," she said.

Sara nodded, unable to speak.

"Grandfather Frank told me they died in an accident. He showed me their graves in the Thunder Lake Cemetery. Whenever I asked Josh about them, he'd snap at me and say, 'I don't remember!' But he must have remembered *something*. He was five when they died."

Suddenly Jessie started crying again. The wind howled and shook the tower window. Sara took a deep breath, then reached for Josh's notebook, opening it to the first page. She recognized his printing.

"Go ahead, read it," said Jessie. "It starts about a year ago. And it ends on the night . . . the night he killed himself."

Sara's hands were shaking. She stared down at the page, afraid to read Josh's last words.

What was he thinking when he jumped to his death? What was he feeling? Why did he do it? Why didn't he talk to me?

Sara suddenly realized she was holding Josh's deep--

est, darkest secrets in her hands—the things he could never, ever, tell her.

And she was terrified.

Do I really want to know the truth?

She looked down at the date on the first page. It was last October, when she and Josh fell in love.

Sara's eyes filled with tears. She heard her own heart pounding, as loudly as the wind lashing at the tower. She looked up as the window rattled in its frame, and saw a dim flash of lightning in the distant mountains. She took another breath.

And through her tears, she began to read . . .

6

The Last Words of Joshua Frank

From the pages of Josh's notebook . . .

I never had a diary before. Not because I think it's a girl thing. I don't care about that. It's just that I've always expressed my feelings in music.

But today, some things happened that are too weird for a song. It's love and death stuff, and it scares me. I have to write it down—or else I'll go crazy.

Anyway, here's what happened.

October 15
What a day. I guess you could call it my day of discovery. Two discoveries, really—one in the heart and one in the head.

The first discovery happened in the highest point of the mansion. I came home from school and threw my books on the bed. A piece of paper slipped out of my biology book, and I knew it wasn't mine. I picked it up, opened it, and couldn't believe my eyes. It was a love letter from Sara Watkins!

Sara is my lab partner at school, and she's beautiful and brilliant, too. She's the school science whiz—and the only reason I'm getting an A in biology. She always seemed a little too cold and rational, but I was determined to break through and find the warmth inside. I played my music for her and told her jokes. I teased her and flirted with her.

And now, in her letter, she says she loves me.

I feel so happy I could scream. And for the first time in my life, I feel like writing a love song. A mushy, gushy love song just like the kind I used to make fun of. In the past, it was easy to mock something I didn't know and couldn't have. But now I feel like shouting it out to the whole world . . .

I'm in love with Sara Watkins!

The second discovery happened in the lowest depths of the mansion. I wanted to give Sara something special—a token of our love—and I knew the perfect gift. It was a gold ring that belonged to my mother, a Frank family heirloom with the old family crest on it. First, I stole the house keys from Grandfather Frank and searched my parents' bedroom, which was locked. I couldn't find the ring. Then I remembered that Grandfather Frank had moved some of their belongings into the basement. So I headed down into that musty old cellar with a flashlight. And I still can't believe what I found there.

The basement used to be a kitchen years ago. The drawers were filled with family possessions, but I couldn't find the ring. I was ready to give up the search when I decided to try Grandfather's keys on

the giant chrome door of the old freezer. I found
the key and opened the door. The freezer was still
working!

I shined the flashlight into the icy mist and stepped
inside. The freezer was empty—except for one big
block of ice on a shelf. I looked closer, holding up
the light, and I almost screamed.

Frozen in the ice was a human head.

Well, not exactly human. It was the ugliest thing
I'd ever seen in my life. The skull was cracked and
sewn up, the face all covered with stitches. The skin
was half rotted, the lips were black, and the eyes were
cold and green and hollow. Two steel bolts jutted out
from its neck.

It looked like the monster from an old Frankenstein
movie!

And here's the really weird part—something inside
of me told me it really *was* the Frankenstein monster.
I felt it in my bones.

I had to know the truth. So I went upstairs and
confronted Grandfather Frank. I told him I found the
thing in the freezer, and I wanted to know everything.
At first, he played dumb. Then I threatened to go to
the police. I knew Grandfather was hiding something
from me. A deep, dark secret. And to my horror, he
told me what it was . . .

The story of Frankenstein is not a legend. It's history. It's true. The head in the freezer belonged to the
original monster . . .

And I am the descendant of Victor Frankenstein.

December 24

It's the night before Christmas. I've just come back from Sara's house, where I had dinner with her family. We sang Christmas carols and exchanged gifts and drank eggnog. It was kind of fun. Spending time with her family—and feeling the warmth and love they share—almost made me forget the horrors that hide within my own home . . .

The house of Frankenstein.

January 5

I just woke up from a nightmare. It started out like a beautiful dream. It was my wedding day. The family mansion was painted white. And Sara was coming down the staircase in her wedding dress. I was so happy. Jessie was the maid of honor, and Grandfather Frank was the best man. I held the gold family ring in my hand and watched Sara descend the stairs. Then it turned into a nightmare . . .

A pair of rotted hands burst through the stairs and grabbed Sara by the ankles. She fell onto the landing. Then another pair of hands ripped through the floorboards, clutching her throat. Sara screamed. The staircase broke away and two monsters pulled themselves up from the basement. It was a man and a woman, both of them zombies, covered with scars and stitches.

I watched in horror as they tore Sara apart limb from limb. And I woke up screaming.

Now—as I put this dream into words—I realize that I recognized those two murderous creatures. They were monsters, created by a Frankenstein, an artificial man and woman who have haunted my dreams since childhood . . .

My father and mother.

February 14

It's Valentine's Day. I never thought I'd be writing words of love in a card covered with hearts and roses. But I can't help the way I feel about Sara.

Unfortunately, I can't help the way I feel about myself, either. I can't stop these feelings of dread that torture me night after night. It's almost as if something is growing inside of me. Something that should be kept locked up in a cage. Something evil . . .

I think I'm losing my mind.

March 30

A weird thing happened in gym class today. We were playing softball. It was my turn at bat, and I stepped up to the plate. Moose Morgan, the school jock, was teasing me because I struck out two innings ago. He yelled something nasty at me. And—I don't know—I exploded. I screamed and charged at him with the baseball bat. Everyone was laughing as I chased him around the field. I don't know what came over me. Before I knew it, I had him cornered against the chain-link fence. Then everything turned red. I roared like an animal and threw the bat with all my might.

Moose ducked down, the bat flew over his head— and tore a hole through the fence! I don't know where

I got the strength to do that. It must have been the power of my rage. Pure blind rage. I don't know where it came from. But one thing I know . . .

I would have killed him if I had the chance.

April 12

Every day I feel my body changing—growing stronger and wilder. Strange, dark thoughts fill my head. I think I'm losing control. I sit at my desk at school and look around at my classmates. They seem like aliens to me, a whole different species. But then I realize that I'm the strange one . . . I'm the freak . . .

What's happening to me?

May 29

I took Sara to Lovers' Lane tonight. It was a disaster. Usually, I feel tender when I'm with her. I hold her and kiss her. I whisper my feelings in her ear. But tonight, on that dusty road on the edge of the lake, I felt no love for Sara—only desire. My body ached with hunger as my hands clawed at her flesh. She cried out in fear. She begged me to slow down. But I wouldn't listen. Her feelings meant nothing to me. I knew what I wanted, and that's all that mattered.

Now, I feel so ashamed. Sara may never forgive me. And without her love, I'm better off dead.

What have I done?

June 2

Tonight was the Junior Prom. Sara and I had a great time! We went on my bike, with Sara riding on the handlebars in her dress! It was a scream! I'm so happy I can't believe it. Sara loves me—and I love her more than anything in the world, even my music. Maybe there's hope for me after all . . .

July 14

Today I tried to kill myself. I found some pills in Grandfather's medicine cabinet. I took them up to my bedroom, locked the door, and swallowed the entire bottle. I did it without a single thought in my head. Like a sleepwalker. After two or three minutes, my stomach started to burn. Then I fell to the floor with convulsions. My guts were heaving in pain, and I coughed and spit up the pills. My head was spinning. The drug was altering my mind. But I didn't feel sleepy or drunk. My thoughts were crystal clear.

I began to remember things. My childhood. I was five years old again. I was sitting on the landing of the stairs, looking down at my mother and father. They were fighting over a baby, my sister Jessie. My mother held the infant in her arms—and my father was trying to kill her. Their faces were gray, and their flesh was rotting away from their bones.

They were monsters.

My own flesh and blood.

My father snatched the baby from my mother's arms and held her high in the air. My mother attacked, scratching his face with her fingernails. They growled and snapped at each other, like two rabid dogs. The baby wailed in terror.

Then Grandfather Frank appeared. He held a hypodermic needle in each hand.

And that's the last thing I remember before I passed out on the floor of my bedroom.

July 20

At last, I know the truth.

Tonight after dinner, I grabbed a large butcher knife from the kitchen and walked to the study in the back of the house. Grandfather Frank was sitting at his desk, reading. His face was blank when he saw the knife in my hand.

"I want to know everything," I said, pointing the blade at his throat. "I want to know what it means to be a Frankenstein. I want to know what happened to my mother and father. And I want to know what's wrong . . . with me."

He said he didn't know what I was talking about. So I showed him . . .

With the tip of the butcher knife, I sliced the palm of my left hand. A trickle of blood flowed across my hand and fell, drop by drop, onto the desk.

The blood wasn't red—it was blue.

Then I held the knife over Grandfather's head. I demanded to know the truth. And I swore that if he didn't tell me everything, I would kill him.

He must have believed me. Because he unlocked his desk with a key and pulled out a short stack of old journals. Then he told me a story so sick and bizarre that I can't believe it's true . . .

Grandfather Frank was once a brilliant surgeon. But in spite of a successful career, he longed for something more—a medical breakthrough that would bring him immortal fame. Then one day, he received news from Switzerland. His father had died and left a small package in his will. It contained the original journal of Victor Frankenstein, his ancestor. Grandfather Frank was ecstatic—for now he possessed the greatest medical discovery of all, the secret of life itself.

And so, he created my mother and father. He built them piece by piece from bodies of the dead, stolen from morgues or robbed from fresh graves. And he named them Adam and Eve.

At first, they were perfect in every way—physically superior and mentally advanced. Then Grandfather Frank decided to take his experiment further. He wanted these creatures to mate, to produce offspring—to spawn a new race of beings unlike any life form on earth . . .

Frankenstein's children.

And so, Jessie and I were born. To Grandfather's surprise, we seemed to be normal, warm-blooded humans. That was his first disappointment. His second was what happened to my parents shortly after Jessie's birth.

They began to deteriorate. Their flesh began to rot, their minds decay. In a matter of months, they were completely out of control. They even tried to kill each other—and their children. Finally, Grandfather Frank had no choice but to destroy them.

End of story.

I looked down at my "grandfather," a weak old man sitting at his desk, and I felt nothing but hate. I wanted to plunge the butcher knife into his chest. I wanted revenge.

At last, I know the truth—and I wish I'd never tried to find it. Because my life is doomed. My love is cursed. And with each passing day, my destiny is clearer . . .

I'm turning into a monster.

August 6

This morning, I lost all the feeling in my left foot. I tried to rub my toes, to warm the gray, dead flesh, and a toenail broke off.

August 12

My handwriting is getting worse. It's hard to control my fingers—or my mind, for that matter. My feet have begun to decay, and the foul rot of death is creeping up my leg. I don't know how to tell Sara. I love her. But my love is overshadowed by madness. Sometimes I think I love Sara so much . . . that I want to kill her.

August 20

I've locked myself in my room with my guitar. I'm writing songs—love songs for Sara. And I'm recording them on the tape deck, so she has something to remember me by.

I can see her house across the lake when I look out the tower window. It gives me hope. But then, I turn my eyes down toward the stone path in front of my house. It's a four-story drop—enough to kill me if I jumped.

September 8

Today was the first day of school. I wore layers of clothes to hide the gray flesh that's rotting from my bones. But I couldn't hide the monstrous feelings in my heart. I verbally attacked my fellow students, and even lashed out at Sara. At least I'm still sane enough to make an important decision—I'm not going back there . . .

The first day of school was also my last.

September 9

Tried to kill Baskerville today. Don't know why. Going crazy. Hate myself. Can't take it any longer. Want to die.

September 10

Tonight I spoke to Sara for the last time.

I told her that we've got to stop seeing each other. She cried. I gave her the Frank family ring. She wanted to know what was wrong. I told her I was cursed, that I was different, that I didn't want to hurt her anymore. Then she left me. And the look of pain on her face will haunt me forever, even in death . . .

Heaven forgive me.

Because tonight I'm going to jump from the tower window.

I'll leave a note for my loved ones. It'll look like another teen suicide. And I have an important message for

(END OF DOCUMENT. FINAL PAGES RIPPED OUT.)

7

Hunger of the Beast

From the diary of Sara Watkins . . .

Sometimes the people you love the most are the ones you know the least.

I thought I knew everything about Josh—but now all of my illusions have been shattered. I used to think the world was filled with good people and with bad people. Now I realize that good and bad exist side by side within us all. Where there is love, there is hate. Where there is happiness, there is pain . . .

And where there is beauty, there is a beast.

On the southern edge of Thunder Lake, a tall, concrete dam stands like an ancient stone god—a man-made Atlas with the weight of the world on its shoulders. The sky assaults the mighty dam with blasts of wind and arrows of rain. The lake swells and presses against its back—a battering ram of water that could flood the earth in a single wave of fury. But the dam is strong, and the reckless forces of nature have been tamed . . .

"Sit, boy! Sit!"

Eddie Perez shouted the command at the big black hound. His voice echoed inside the old grist mill, rising up over the sound of flowing water that turned the mill's waterwheel.

"Sit!"

The dog wasn't impressed by the tone—or volume—of Eddie's voice. Instead of sitting, the huge animal jumped up and licked the boy's face.

"Come on, Baskerville," Eddie pleaded. "I promised Sara I'd run these tests on you. Just let me hook up these wires."

He looked down at Baskerville and wondered what was wrong.

The lightning storm had driven the dog crazy. Its eyes were glowing fiercely, and the long muscles beneath its sleek black fur were pulsating and flexing.

And that howl . . .

Baskerville had tried to echo the thunder in the sky when it passed overhead. And the sound that erupted from the dog's throat was enough to raise the dead.

Eddie shivered.

The storm—and Baskerville's reaction—frightened him. Out here in the old mill, on the edge of the dam, it seemed as if Mother Nature herself were seeking revenge. The mill, after all, was the laboratory of mortals who tried to steal her greatest secrets. The secrets of life and death.

Eddie breathed a sigh of relief when the storm

drifted away into the mountains. Baskerville seemed a little calmer now—but still a little wild.

"Thatta boy, sit."

Eddie crouched down and clamped two thin cables onto the electrodes in Baskerville's neck. The steel knobs jutted out like two spikes, above the dog collar, but they didn't seem to irritate the dog. Even when a spark of electricity crackled and jumped, Baskerville didn't twitch.

"Good boy," said Eddie, standing up slowly so he wouldn't startle the dog. "Stay."

Baskerville froze like a statue. His eyes were fixed on something across the room.

Eddie looked to see what it was . . .

Through the slashes of light that penetrated the walls of the old mill, he saw the internal axle of the waterwheel—turning, spinning, slow and steady. In the corner was a table covered with flasks, beakers, and test tubes. And on the shelves were bandages and gauze, needles and thread, clamps and scalpels . . .

Nothing unusual.

Eddie squinted his eyes, focusing on the shadows across the floorboards. And there it was, small and gray—the thing that captured Baskerville's attention . . .

A mouse.

"Okay, Baskerville," Eddie whispered. "You keep your eye on the mouse, and I'll just run a few tests."

He walked over to the computer terminal and sat down. He punched a few keys, and the screen blinked to life.

"Let's see now," Eddie mumbled to himself.

"Ten twenty-five examination, Baskerville, hound dog. Check. Run standard physical. Begin . . ."

A series of numbers and charts flashed across the computer screen. Eddie pressed the keys as each test was evaluated, then entered the data into the memory.

"Nervous system, check . . . heart rate, check . . . blood pressure, check . . ."

In a matter of minutes, the tests were completed, and Eddie typed in the command to print out a hard copy of the results. The computer printer clicked and whirred, then produced the exam, page by page.

Eddie looked up from his work. Baskerville was still sitting in the middle of the room—still staring at the mouse and licking his chops hungrily.

Then Eddie noticed the big plastic bowl on the floor next to Baskerville . . .

It was filled with dog food.

"If you're so hungry, why don't you eat some of your food?" Eddie said softly. "You haven't touched a bite since . . ."

Since Josh, your master, strangled you to death.

Suddenly Eddie felt cold. The autumn wind reached down from the rafters of the mill, touching the back of his neck with icy fingers of air. Eddie looked up through the hole in the arched ceiling, where he could see the broken windows of the watchtower . . .

Where the nightmare was born.

Eddie closed his eyes and remembered Josh's corpse hanging from chains in the watchtower, and lightning striking the kites that Eddie had sent up into the storm.

And now Eddie wondered why he took part in such a gruesome experiment.

Why did he help Sara steal body parts from the morgue? Why did he hook up computers and generators to her boyfriend's corpse? Why did he risk his own life for the ultimate challenge of death?

The answer was simple . . .

Sara.

Eddie helped create a monster because that's what Sara wanted. It was the only way he knew to make friends with her. And Eddie desperately needed friends.

Oh, yeah? he thought. What about Kiki Austin? She seems to like me.

The thought didn't make him feel any better. In fact, it filled him with dread. The date was probably one of Heather's pranks. Even if it wasn't, what would he say to Kiki? What would he wear?

Eddie had never been on a real date before.

The fact that it was the Halloween Dance only made it worse. Kiki said she was going as a fairy princess—and told him to wear something appropriate.

Like what? Eddie wondered. A fairy *prince* costume?

Eddie's daydream was shattered in a flash . . .

Because Baskerville howled like a demon—and dashed across the room after the mouse.

The wires at his throat stretched and snapped away from the electrodes in a shower of sparks. The steel-chain leash tightened and ripped the dog collar in half. And Baskerville shot across the room like a bullet—a blur of black fur and snarling teeth.

"Baskerville!"

Eddie shouted out, but he didn't know why. Nothing could stop that dog once he started running, and hunting, and feasting . . .

The mouse didn't stand a chance.

It scurried across the floorboards, racing for its life. But Baskerville was too fast. He was on top of the tiny rodent in the blink of an eye, his hungry jaws closing down and snapping shut before the mouse had any idea it had lost the race.

Eddie watched in horror. He saw the fiery gleam in the dog's black eyes as it tilted back its head, gnawing, chomping, gulping down its prey, then licking its teeth and wagging its tail.

It all happened so fast, Eddie would have missed it if he blinked his eyes.

He glanced down at the bowl of dog food on the floor. Then he looked at Baskerville and whispered, "What's wrong with you?"

Silly question, Eddie thought. The dog's a living corpse, just like his master who strangled him to death.

He stared at the empty lab table and thought about the nightmares he and Sara and Jessie had created. The only good thing to come out of all this was their friendship—and Eddie's feelings for Sara . . .

But even that was a nightmare, too.

Suddenly his thoughts were broken by a loud knock on the door. Eddie jumped. "Who is it?"

"Me and Jessie! Let us in!"

It was Sara. Eddie's heart almost stopped. But that's how he felt every time he saw her.

He flung open the door. Sara and Jessie burst into the room, slamming the door behind them. Their faces were flushed, their cheeks stained with tears.

"Eddie . . ."

Sara gasped for air and collapsed into the boy's arms. Her heart was pounding. Eddie could feel it against his chest. He held her tight and glanced at Jessie, who looked like she was ready to faint.

"What's wrong?" he asked.

Jessie turned around and walked to a chair in the corner of the room. She fell back into the seat, pulling up her legs and hugging her knees. She started to cry.

Sara trembled in Eddie's arms. "It's . . . something about Josh . . ."

"Did he attack you? Are you all right?" Eddie felt a tide of rage sweep through him.

"No, he didn't attack me . . ." Sara wept as she tried to speak. "None of it is Josh's fault . . . He was born that way . . ."

Eddie frowned. "What do you mean?"

Sara took a deep breath. "He was . . . always . . . always . . ." Her voice broke off into sobs.

Eddie looked at Jessie in the corner. She lifted her head and pushed a strand of black hair out of her eyes. Then she stood up slowly and spoke.

"She's trying to tell you that my brother was always a monster," Jessie said. "And maybe I am, too."

The thing in the cage heard footsteps.

Someone was coming down the stairs, crossing the

first room of the basement, and opening the door. The creature looked up to see who it was . . .

The old man.

The creature didn't like the old man. Not for any particular reason. The old man never hurt him. He never hit him with a wooden bat. Not like that boy who chased the creature up to the roof of the school. The creature didn't like the boy, either. So he threw him off the roof.

The creature wanted to throw the old man off the roof, too. He didn't know why.

Now the old man was shouting at him, yelling and waving something in the air.

It was a notebook.

My notebook.

The creature recognized it. It belonged to him when he was alive. And it was very special.

But the old man hated the notebook—and hated the creature it belonged to. He ranted and raved and called the creature names. He walked back and forth outside the cage, slapping the notebook against the bars. And in his angry stream of words, the old man said something that sounded familiar to the creature . . .

" . . . grandson . . ."

The word sparked a tiny chain reaction in the creature's brain . . . igniting a single memory . . . inspiring a simple thought . . . and spawning a terrible realization . . .

The creature knew who the old man was.

Grandfather.

And the creature knew what the old man had done.

Raised the dead.

The thing in the cage growled at the old man, then stood and threw himself against the bars. The old man backed away in fear. He mumbled something to the creature. Then he turned and walked out of the basement, slamming the door behind him.

The creature roared.

He grasped the bars of the cage with his huge, powerful hands, pulled with all his strength, multiplied by the fury of his rage, his pain, his anguish . . .

And the bars began to bend.

"I'm a monster! Don't you understand?"

Jessie sat on the floor of the old grist mill, her hands wrapped around Baskerville's neck. The dog's electrodes brushed against her arm. The cold steel sent a chill through her body.

"Josh and I are the children of monsters," she went on. "Then we raised Josh from the dead and created a double monster."

She started to cry again. The black hound licked away her tears. She stared coldly at the steel knobs on either side of the dog's throat.

"And what about Baskerville?" she said. "Josh strangled him, and now we've turned him into a monster, too."

Sara looked at Eddie in despair. "Did you run the tests on Baskerville?"

Eddie nodded and reached for the hard copy of the computer evaluation. "Here," he said, handing it to Sara.

She took the papers and flipped through them

quickly. "Well," she said. "His reflexes, strength, and blood pressure are accelerated. The storm seems to have doubled his metabolism and strength. But at least he seems to be acting normal."

Eddie cleared his throat. "Not exactly," he said.

Sara and Jessie looked up, their eyes burning with curiosity.

Eddie explained. "The storm drove him nuts. You should have heard him howl."

"I did," said Sara.

"Me, too," said Jessie.

Eddie went on. "Then he broke his chain when he ran across the room. But even before that . . . before the storm . . . he's been a little strange. He hasn't eaten his dog food since we resurrected him."

"That's impossible," said Sara. "He must have eaten *something*."

Eddie looked down at the dog in Jessie's arms. "He's been killing and eating mice."

"Mice?" said Jessie.

"Yeah . . . He goes crazy when he sees one. I've never seen a dog move so fast."

"That's weird," said Jessie. "Baskerville never chased animals before. In fact, he used to be terrified of cats and squirrels and rabbits . . . He was never much of a hunting dog."

Eddie shrugged his shoulders. "He is now."

Sara laid the test results on the lab table and paced back and forth. Her mind was filled with strange and terrifying information . . .

Death and resurrection. Reanimated parents. A son turning monstrous. A dog brought back to life.

"The only conclusion I can make," she said at last, "is that artificial life unleashes the animal instincts that already exist."

Jessie stroked Baskerville's ears. "What about me?" she asked. "Will I turn into a monster, too?"

Sara looked into Jessie's eyes and sighed. The poor girl was terrified, and Sara couldn't think of anything to say that would make her feel better.

"I don't know, Jessie," she whispered slowly. "I really don't know."

Jessie's eyes filled with tears. "Maybe we should ask Grandfather . . ."

A shadow crossed Sara's face. "I'm not sure, Jessie," she said, hesitating. "I'm not sure I trust your grandfather."

Suddenly the door of the mill swung open and slammed against the wall.

Sara, Jessie, and Eddie almost jumped out of their skin. Their heads snapped around, their eyes focusing on the open doorway. There, standing in the rain, was a tall, gaunt figure . . .

It was Grandfather Frank.

And he was holding Josh's notebook.

8

Force of Nature

From the diary of Sara Watkins . . .

Sometimes I blame myself for everything. Sometimes I blame Grandfather Frank. And other times I feel that it's nobody's fault—the horrors of life are caused by forces of nature out of our control.

But isn't every human being also a force of nature? Shouldn't each of us take responsibility for the things we do—and the things we create?

I don't know the answers to these questions. But I know one thing . . .

If Josh ever broke out of his cage—and unleashed his fury upon the world—I would plead guilty to every unspeakable crime he committed.

The storm disappeared behind the mountains of Thunder Lake, slipping away as quickly as it struck.

But the creature still felt its power—the flash of lightning and roar of thunder—pulsing through his monstrous limbs. He grasped the bars of the cage and pulled as hard as he could.

The bars opened wider—wide enough to pull his body out of the cage.

The creature grunted. A wave of electrical power surged through his nerves, his muscles, his brain. He stepped through the bars, one foot at a time.

And he was free.

His hair hung down in his eyes, but his vision seemed clearer, his mind focused on a single dark thought . . .

Revenge.

He staggered toward the door and pushed. It was locked. So he pushed harder—and harder—until the door splintered apart against his huge hands, the boards cracking and smashing to the floor.

And the creature stepped through.

He stood in the first basement room, his eyes turning in their sockets. They stopped on the huge chrome door against the far wall. The freezer . . .

His brain wriggled in his skull.

And he stumbled forward, reaching out for the steel handle of the freezer. His hands gripped the latch, and he wrenched it open, shattering the lock on the door.

Icy mist poured out of the small chamber. The creature growled. Something—a lost memory—urged him forward into the freezer. His eyes glowed with curiosity. He looked through the mist. And he saw it . . .

The monstrous head in a block of ice.

Josh leaned closer and pressed his hand against the ice. It was so cold, he pulled away. Then he grunted and touched it again.

Inside the ice, the horrible face seemed to be staring at Josh—those hideous dead eyes piercing Josh's soul.

It was so ugly, that face, twisted and covered with scars.

Josh reached up and touched his own face.

It, too, was twisted and covered with scars.

His eyes filling with tears, Josh roared and backed away from the monstrous head frozen in ice. He staggered out of the freezer. He opened his mouth and unleashed a sad cry of anguish and pain. Then he turned and looked toward the basement stairs, his mind reeling . . .

Revenge.

Staggering up the stairs, the creature growled and sobbed. The door at the top wasn't locked. He pushed it open easily and stepped into the dark entry hall of the mansion.

He knew what he needed to do.

Find Grandfather.

The door to Grandfather Frank's study was closed. Josh walked slowly down the hall and stopped outside the door. He listened. Silence. Then he pushed the door open and slammed it against the wall.

There was no one in the study. Just an empty desk in the middle of the room and shelves of dusty books.

The creature frowned.

Where was Grandfather?

The wind whistled around the corners of the house, piercing the cracks and crevices in the ancient walls. The creature listened. The voice of the wind was a lonely sound. A sound that seemed to cry out to the creature . . .

He staggered toward the desk and looked down at Grandfather Frank's papers. With a gray, clumsy hand, he pushed the papers across the desk, searching for the message he had left for Grandfather on the night he killed himself . . .

It was Josh's final warning.

None of the papers on the desk looked familiar to the creature. So he opened the drawers, one by one. Nothing.

Then he tried the bottom drawer. It was locked.

Josh growled and wrenched it open.

There, on the bottom of the drawer, was a black leather-bound journal—a dusty, ancient document that touched a nerve deep within the creature.

What was it?

He opened the cover and studied the words scrawled on the first page . . .

"A Study in the Creation of Life."

Then, in curled handwriting, was the name "Victor Frankenstein."

The creature, however, could not read the words. His brain couldn't grasp the meaning of these strange shapes on paper. But he knew it wasn't what he was looking for . . .

It wasn't the message.

He closed the drawer and walked slowly out of the study. The house was dark, the draft cold and insistent. Somewhere upstairs, a window rattled. The creature lifted his head and looked up into the darkness of the grand staircase.

And he started to climb the steps.

Where was Grandfather?

On the second floor, he stopped. Somewhere in his mind, he knew that Grandfather slept here—in the first room down the hall.

The creature stepped forward, bandages shredding away from his arms and legs. The thunderstorm had infused his muscles with new life, new strength. They bulged against his tight, gray flesh and stretched his stitches to the breaking point.

It was a feeling of pleasure—and of pain.

Josh walked to Grandfather Frank's bedroom door and pushed it open.

The room was dark and silent. The bed was empty. Grandfather was not there.

The creature stepped inside, looked around, then walked to the giant dresser against the wall. He reached for the handle of a drawer . . .

And he froze.

Because he saw his reflection in the huge mirror above the dresser.

No . . .

The creature had seen his face only once before— reflected in Sara's bedroom window.

But this was worse.

The image was sharper, clearer—and so much more horrifying.

No . . .

His face was hideous, a broken mask of scars and stitches and gray, dead flesh, stretched tight over a large, twisted skull. His green, glowing eyes bulged within dark, hollow sockets. His hair was a dirty, tangled mass of curls, and his forehead was pierced by two steel clamps.

No . . .

First, he wept. Then, he tilted back his head and roared in pain and anguish and rage . . .

"NOOOO!"

Pounding his fist against the dresser, Josh screamed and sobbed. He reached down and ripped open a drawer, the contents spilling at his feet.

Suddenly he stopped.

Because, there on the floor was what he was looking for . . .

The message.

Slowly, he crouched down and picked up the crumpled envelope. He recognized the printing—it was his own—and he knew what the strange shapes on the envelope said . . .

For Grandfather.

It was Josh's warning.

He opened the envelope and stared at the writing on the page . . .

Grandfather,

Tonight, I'm going to kill myself. I think you know why.

Day by day I am turning into a monster—like my parents. But I refuse to be part of your sick experiments any longer. I'm not a laboratory mouse. I'm a human being. How dare you play with life and death as if it were a game! You brought Jessie and me into this world—cursed from the day we were born. If this is a game, you're going to lose. Because I refuse to be your pawn.

As my body and mind rot away, I realize that I have three choices:

I can let science try to cure me. I can let nature take its course. Or I can let death have the final word.

Well, I've made my choice.

And if you dare to resurrect me from the dead, I promise you this—I'll hunt you down and kill you if it's the last thing I do.

I'll show you just how monstrous I really am.

Because I am no longer Joshua Frank. I am a force of nature beyond your control.

Resurrect me—and die.

> Joshua Frank,
> The Last of the Frankensteins

The creature stared down at the words on the page. He couldn't read the message—but he understood it clearly, deep in his heart and soul . . .

Grandfather must die.

Revenge.

Bending down, he picked up the drawer and clumsily pushed it back into the dresser. He replaced its contents carefully, and closed it.

He wanted to surprise Grandfather.

Clutching the message in his hand, the creature turned and walked out of the room, into the hallway. He listened to the sounds of the empty house . . .

Just the wind.

And he climbed the stairs, up, higher—to the top floor of the mansion . . .

His bedroom.

He opened the door and walked inside. Everything was exactly how he had left it. His bed, his books, his posters, his music stand . . .

He started to weep.

Because this was a world he had lost forever—the world of the living.

The tower window rattled in its frame, startling the creature. He looked up, then walked toward it.

He stared out into the night. The moon was rising, its pale light illuminating the town . . .

The lake. The dam. The old mill.

And Sara's house . . .

The tears flowed down Josh's face, gliding along the stitches and scars. He pressed his hand against the glass, whispering . . .

"Sa . . . ra."

And his heart—that strange alien thing in his chest—was filled with pain.

He lowered his eyes and saw the stone path leading up to the mansion. He remembered the night he killed himself—standing on the window ledge, staring down at the ground, tears in his eyes, Sara's name on his lips . . .

Then jumping, headfirst, leaping, falling . . .

And the stone path rushing toward him, like death with open arms, ready to embrace him . . .

Falling, falling . . .

Then darkness.

The creature touched the windowpane of the tower and closed his eyes.

It should have ended there—in darkness.

But there was more.

There was thunder and rain . . .

And lightning.

Lightning in his brain . . . lightning in his heart . . . lightning in his soul . . .

And suddenly he was alive.

Again.

The creature leaned against the window frame, his tears blurring his vision. He blinked his eyes, and everything was clear again.

His sorrow turned to rage. And his rage was focused on one person . . .

Grandfather.

And one thought . . .

Revenge.

He looked out the window and noticed a small hill in the distance a dark and bleak place marked with gray stones and statues and crosses . . .

It was Thunder Lake Cemetery.

And it was where Grandfather Frank had buried Josh's mother and father.

The creature knew what a graveyard was, and he knew who belonged there . . .

The dead.

Like himself. And his parents.

He stared down at the gravestones and felt a strange longing in his heart . . .

He wanted to see his mom and dad.

Josh had never felt this way before, even when he was alive. But something deep inside of him yearned for the mother and father he barely knew.

The creature pulled himself away from the window.

Then he turned and staggered down the stairs of the mansion, out the front door, and along the edge of the lake . . .

To the cemetery.

9

Skeletons in the Closet

From the secret journal of Professor Frank . . .

Some people would call me a monster.

I have brought the dead to life. I named them Adam and Eve, and told them to be fruitful and multiply. Then I studied their living offspring—Josh and Jessie—as if they were insects on a slide.

Some of this is true. But I swear I raised Josh and Jessie as my own flesh and blood. Because they are more than just skeletons in the family closet. They are the true and final descendants of that infamous experiment that spawned a terrible legend . . .

They are truly Frankenstein's children.

And they are mine—forever.

The waterwheel of the old mill turned as slowly and surely as the endless circle of life itself. The rippling force of the lake pushed against the dam and flowed through a small concrete channel, its energy absorbed by the moss-covered paddles of the wheel. The wooden circle turned, the water spilled forth, and plunged—hundreds of feet into the black valley beyond the dam.

Sara listened to the creaking of the wheel's axle within the dam. And she realized something . . .

The lake was life. The valley was death. And the mill was the mysterious link that harnessed the powers of both.

It was where life and death became one.

Sara shivered.

Grandfather Frank saw her tremble as he took a seat in the corner—and smiled. Eddie and Jessie gathered around him on the floor, their hands stretched out for Sara to join them.

Her stomach was in knots. She held the hands of her two best friends and sat on the wooden planks between them.

Grandfather Frank cleared his throat.

"I found this notebook on Josh's bed," he began, clutching the object in his gnarled hands. "And I'm sure you've read it."

Sara nodded slowly. Jessie swallowed her sobs.

"So you know the story of Adam and Eve," he said, choosing his words carefully. "But you only know the story from Josh's point of view. Not mine. And that's why I came here. To tell you everything. Everything you want to know."

Sara's heart was pounding. She squeezed Jessie's hand and asked a question. "Why should we believe you? After all, you convinced me to raise Josh from the dead when you knew there were complications.

You're a liar, Professor Frank."

The old man smiled. "My dear Sara," he said. "Do you think I would have resurrected him if I knew it would turn out so tragically? If you don't believe my story, I'll gladly show you my private journals. I've kept documents of everything . . . from the moment I created Adam and Eve."

Sara frowned. She didn't trust him, but what choice did she have.

"Okay," she said, "tell us your story."

Grandfather Frank nodded politely and leaned back in his chair. Then he closed his eyes. And as he began to speak, Sara's awareness of her surroundings—the old mill, the waterwheel, the howling wind—seemed to fade away like a lost memory.

And Grandfather Frank's voice filled her senses . . .

"In the beginning, I created Adam and Eve.

"I found my raw materials in graveyards and morgues. I was a renowned surgeon, you must understand, and all of the remains of life and death were at my fingertips.

"You may ask me why. Why did I choose to carry on these horrible, ghastly experiments? Why did I follow in the cursed footsteps of my ancestor, Victor Frankenstein? The answer is simple. I am first and foremost a doctor, dedicated to saving lives. And what medical discovery could possibly be more important than the reversal of death? You may disapprove of me, you may condemn me, but I swear . . . my intentions were always for the benefit of mankind.

"Still, I realized the controversial nature of my experiments. And I performed my ghoulish tasks far from prying eyes. I came to Thunder Lake, Pennsylvania, because it is such a small, quiet town. By day, I worked as chief of surgery at the county hospital. But by night, I labored over the greatest mysteries of nature.

"Ah, Adam and Eve . . . they were so perfect in their construction, so lovely to the eye, so uplifting for the soul. I used only the freshest materials. I gave them perfect bones, perfect muscles, perfect brains.

"These mangled hands of mine will never again create such exquisite work.

"Finally, I was ready to bring them to life. I built my laboratory in the highest tower of the mansion, which later became Josh's bedroom. I erected a fifty-foot lightning rod above the tower. And I waited for the storm to come.

"And come it did. Heaven sent its lightning, like vengeful arrows, down upon me. They struck the rod. Once. Twice. And Adam and Eve were born.

"I was ecstatic, drunk with the victory of life over death. My creations were like gods upon the earth. Strong. Beautiful. Brilliant. They were like giant children, thirsty for knowledge and culture, which I supplied them in great abundance. My experiment was a smashing success.

"But then, Adam and Eve began to want more. More knowledge, more experience, than I could ever give them. They wanted to have children of their own.

"How could I refuse them? They could have asked for the moon and the stars, and I would have tried to pull them down from the sky. Adam and Eve were the children I never had. And why should I refuse them the same joys of parenthood that they had brought to me?

"And so Josh was born. A beautiful, perfect, living, breathing baby boy. To my surprise, his blood was red and warm, not blue and cold like the artificial brew that flowed through his parents' veins. He was such a lovely child that I allowed Adam and Eve to spawn yet another. A few years later, Jessie was born.

"Which brings me to the tragic part of the story. I was ready to reveal my discovery to the world. What a triumph I had accomplished! Surely, I would win the Nobel Prize in Medicine! But as I prepared my subjects for my first public announcement to the medical community, I noticed something very disturbing.

"Adam and Eve were beginning to decay.

"Their flesh was rotting, cell by cell, and I couldn't do anything to stop it. Even their brains were decaying at an alarming rate. They grew violent, and monstrous. They tried to kill their own children, and myself as well.

"I had no choice but to build two cages in the basement. The hard part was trying to lock them in these cages. First, I drugged their food. Then I dragged them down to the basement. Just as I was about to lock the cages, Adam woke up—and attacked me.

"I fought for my life. He was an animal, a demonic beast from hell itself. I managed to slam the door of the cage, but Adam held tight to my left hand. He clawed my fingers with his razor-sharp nails. Then, he used his teeth . . .

"I screamed in agony and reached for the other cage to pull myself away. But Eve was there behind the bars—and she grabbed my right hand and started biting and clawing, just like her infernal husband.

"I was pulled back and forth, stretched between the two cages, as these vicious creatures gnawed at my hands. The hands of a surgeon! The hands that fed them! The hands that brought them to life! I hung there, between them, crucified . . .

"Until finally I passed out.

"When I awoke, most of the skin had been torn from my hands. I screamed as I looked down at the ends of my wrists and saw two lifeless, bloody clumps of raw meat.

"I thought my life was ruined. How could I save Adam and Eve . . . how could I prepare a cure for their bodily decay . . . when my hands were useless? In despair, I watched them rot away before my eyes, day after day.

"And the only thing that brought joy or hope into my life was Josh and Jessie. They were the angels who offered salvation to my bedeviled soul.

"For the next fifteen years, I watched them carefully. I wanted to make sure they were healthy and happy. But in the back of my mind, I feared that someday they, too—like their parents—would rot away as living corpses. I swore to myself that I wouldn't let that happen. I watched them grow up, year after year. I was thrilled when Josh found a girlfriend with an interest in science. I even fantasized that someday

Sara would carry on the Frankenstein tradition.

"Then the unthinkable happened. Josh killed himself. I had no idea why. I never saw it coming. He was a moody boy, yes, but Sara had brought light to his world. Why would he kill himself? I thought the heavens were punishing me for stealing their secrets. And that made me angry! I wanted to defy the heavens once again! If only my hands could perform the surgery!

"And that's when I saw the pain in Sara's eyes . . . pain that mirrored my own. And I knew there was hope. I knew she could do it for me . . .

"I knew that Josh would live again."

Grandfather Frank lowered his head and closed his eyes. Sara and Jessie brushed away their tears, and Eddie rubbed the top of Baskerville's head.

No one said anything for a while—they were hypnotized by the steady turning of the waterwheel. Finally, Sara leaned forward.

"Are you telling me that you didn't know Josh was turning into a monster when he killed himself?" she asked.

"That is correct," said Grandfather Frank.

Sara frowned. "But in Josh's notebook, he said that he cut his hand with a knife and showed you his blood. It was blue."

The old man smiled. "As a scientist, Sara, I'm sure you know that arterial blood—blood from an artery, as opposed to a vein—is bluish in color."

Sara nodded. "So you thought that Josh had cut an artery?"

"Exactly."

Sara shifted on the floor and glanced at Jessie and Eddie. They seemed to believe him. She turned and studied Grandfather Frank's pale, lined face.

He's lying, she thought.

And she asked another question. "Why were you willing to reanimate Josh when you knew that his parents had rotted away?"

Grandfather Frank cleared his throat. "Even though I could no longer perform surgery, I was perfectly capable of theoretical research. For fifteen years I worked on the formula for artificial blood. I believe I have solved the problem. Josh will not decay."

Baskerville squeezed between the two girls and licked Jessie's face. Jessie smiled as she rubbed the dog's ears.

"So Baskerville's going to be okay?" Jessie asked.

"I guarantee it," said Grandfather Frank.

Jessie cheered. "You hear that, pooch?" she said to the giant hound. "You're new and improved."

Then a shadow crossed Jessie's face—and tears filled her eyes.

"Grandfather," she whispered. "What about me? Am I going to turn into a monster?"

The old man shifted in his chair and stared up at the turning axle of the waterwheel. Sara and Eddie glanced at each other. They were both thinking the same thing . . .

He doesn't know.

"Jessie, my dear," said the old man. "You're a

perfectly normal—and healthy—young lady."

"Josh was healthy and normal, too," said Jessie. "But he was rotting away like a corpse! You read his notebook!"

"Perhaps he was imagining things."

"Perhaps he was telling the truth!"

"Jessie, calm down . . ."

"That's easy for you to say! You're not the one who's going to turn into a monster!"

"Jessie! Listen to me!" said the old man firmly. "I promise you, there are ways to stop this. If it becomes necessary, I'll perform a blood transfusion. But in the meantime, there's nothing to do but wait."

Jessie blinked her eyes. "Wait?"

"Yes. Wait for the first signs of decay. It may not happen for a month, a year, a decade . . . It may never happen at all. But you have no other choice. You have to wait."

Jessie sighed. "Wait, huh? What a thing to wait for. It sounds worse than puberty."

Grandfather Frank smiled bitterly. Then he stood up. "I'm very tired, children. I hope I've answered all of your questions."

Sara cleared her throat. "Professor Frank?" she said. "I have another question."

The old man stopped and turned. "Yes?"

"Whatever happened to Adam and Eve? How did they finally die?"

Grandfather Frank looked down at the floor. "I'm afraid they simply rotted away in their cages."

Sara saw something flash in the old man's eyes— a memory too painful to reveal. She knew he wasn't telling the whole story.

Maybe he killed them, she thought. Or maybe they're still alive.

"Where are they now?" she asked.

Grandfather Frank smirked and turned away. "The boneyard, of course," he answered, walking toward the door.

"The boneyard?"

"Yes, yes!" he said impatiently. "Thunder Lake Cemetery. Where all the dead things go."

‡·|·|·|·|·|·|·|·|·|·|·|·|·|·|·|·|·|·|·|·|·|·|·|·|·|·|·|·‡

10

The Boneyard

From the Thunder Lake High School newspaper *The Weekly Thunder* . . .

> ### *TOMBSTONE TIPPERS, BEWARE!*
> *If you think it's fun to party in a graveyard—look out. Officer Colker of the Thunder Lake Police Department is prepared to press charges against all trespassers in Thunder Lake Cemetery. "Some kids might think it's funny to knock over gravestones," said Officer Colker, "but it's vandalism of the worst sort. Last year, six stones were tipped over. This year, I plan to arrest anyone who even steps foot in that cemetery after hours."*
>
> *So, show a little respect for the dead—and stay out of the boneyard!! You never know. If the law doesn't catch you, maybe something dead will . . .*

There's nothing like a cemetery after dark.

The gravestones rise up like bone-white fingers,

pointing bitterly at the heavens above. Marble angels stare down at the earth with cold stone eyes. And the gray mausoleum walls weep and wail in silence.

The living call it a place of eternal slumber. But in Thunder Lake Cemetery, nothing sleeps and nothing dreams.

The dead are restless.

The creature felt their presence as he staggered past the gravestones, hearing the cries of lost souls beneath the soft, damp earth. He trembled—not with fear—but with a terrible excitement. For the first time since his creation, the monster felt a strange sense of belonging. At last, he was with his own kind, among the dead . . .

He was coming home.

A gentle wind raced around the tombstones and crypts, whistling a song that touched the creature's soul. Autumn leaves, plucked from their branches, danced and fell to the earth, covering the graves in a golden blanket of death and decay.

Yes, he was home, at last.

A tear rolled down the creature's face. And somewhere, deep in his broken mind, he remembered a phrase from his past—words that were spoken when his mother and father were placed in the earth . . .

Ashes to ashes, dust to dust.

The creature felt the death surging through his long limbs, pulsing in his heart and tugging at his soul. He knew he was born out of death. And he knew that he must someday return . . .

Mother . . . Father . . .

He turned his massive head back and forth, search-

ing the cemetery with his sunken eyes. He reached
back into his mind and tried to remember where they
were buried. Then he stumbled toward the edge of
the graveyard, compelled by instinct like an animal
finding its way home.

Finally, he saw it—a tall, broad headstone with two
names carved in marble . . .

In memory of Adam and Eve Frank.

With a sudden burst of emotion, the creature threw
himself onto the grave and wept. His fingers reached
up to stroke the carvings on the stone. His cracked lips
kissed the wet leaves and dirt. And his heart nearly
exploded with joy.

He had found them. His mother and father. The
only ones who would ever understand.

He wanted them and needed them, more than anything in the world. For they, too, were born in death.
They, too, had suffered in life.

The creature embraced the sunken earth of his parents' grave, sobbing in pain and heartache. Gold-
en dead leaves swirled over his head and the wind
howled a warning in his ear. But the creature no
longer cared about the wind or the leaves or anything
in this world—the world of the living . . .

He wanted to return to the world of the dead.

He longed to join his mother and father—to crawl
down into the earth, into their caskets, curling up
between them, holding them, loving them forever.

And they would love him, too.

Love . . .

A flash of distant lightning illuminated the sky,
and the creature raised his fist and cursed that which

brought him to life. He sobbed in rage and dropped his head, staring at the grave of his long-lost mother and father . . .

And with tears in his eyes, he began to dig.

<hr>

"I hate graveyards!" said Kiki Austin, standing at the gates of Thunder Lake Cemetery.

"Why?" asked Jimbo. "Because it's filled with slimy, rotten *corpses* crawling with flesh-eating *worms*?"

His buddy, Crusher, laughed and slapped Jimbo's back. Heather Leigh Clark leaned against the cemetery gate, rolling her eyes.

"Come on," she said. "Let's go find a place to party before the cops find us."

Then the blond cheerleader marched into the graveyard with her head held high. Jimbo and Crusher smirked and followed her—which left Kiki all by herself.

"Hey, guys! Wait for me!" the redhead shouted, running after them.

The darkness engulfed the four teenagers as they walked deeper into the cemetery. The ground was wet from the storm, and their feet sank into the dirt with each step. They headed for the top of the hill, where a tall mausoleum rose up against the night sky.

"Come on," said Crusher. "This tomb has a window we can crawl into."

Kiki squealed. "You want to go inside a crypt?"

"Sure, why not?" said Jimbo. "We're all gonna end up in one sooner or later."

"I'd rather do it later," Kiki muttered.

Heather sighed. "Don't be such a baby, Kiki."

"I'm sorry, but I *hate* graveyards," she said. "And the cops said they'd arrest anyone who trespasses."

"That's what makes it so exciting," said Heather, stepping up to the mausoleum window. "Someone give me a boost."

Jimbo and Crusher tripped over each other, trying to help Heather crawl through the empty window. One by one, they wriggled into the cold, dank crypt. Heather lit a candle she brought in her purse, and Jimbo broke out the liquid refreshments.

Soon, the party was swinging.

"Wanna do a little crypt-kicking?" Jimbo asked the girls.

Heather laughed, and Kiki said, "What's crypt-kicking?"

"Tipping over tombstones," Crusher explained. "Me and Jimbo are world-class crypt-kickers. We knocked over six stones last year. Didn't you read about it in the papers?"

"Oh, yeah," said Kiki.

"Well, whattaya say? Wanna tip some tombs with us?"

"Maybe later," said Heather.

Kiki hugged her knees as she sat on the stone floor and looked around the mausoleum. The candle flickered, and shadows danced and leapt across the white marble walls. "This is creepy," she said softly.

Heather laughed. "I didn't think creepy things bothered you, Kiki," she said. "After all, you agreed to go to the Halloween Dance with Eddie Perez."

"Eddie Perez?" said Jimbo.

"Is he that Puerto Rican computer geek?" asked Crusher.

"Yeah," said Heather. "And he's Kiki's date for Saturday night!"

Crusher and Jimbo howled.

"That nerd's in love with Sara Watkins," said Crusher. "He wrote a poem for her! Jimbo and I saw him write it on his computer. What a loser! He's got the hots for the Ice Witch!"

Heather squinted and smiled. "I thought so," she said.

Jimbo slid next to Kiki and put his arm around her. "You poor thing, dating a nerd," he said. "Why are you doing it?"

"Because Kiki owes me a big favor," said Heather. "I told her parents she was staying at my house last week."

The football players leered and laughed. "So now you're stuck on a date with Eddie Perez!"

Kiki frowned and stared down at the floor of the mausoleum. "He ain't so bad," she whispered.

The others gasped in mock horror.

"He's kind of cute," said Kiki, standing up and walking toward the window. "He looks good with long hair."

"The guy couldn't bench press a lollipop!" said Jimbo.

"So what?" Kiki scowled. "At least he's not a dumb jock."

Jimbo jumped up. "Hey! I think we've been insulted, Crusher!"

Crusher waved it off. "I don't care," he said. "I'd be defensive, too, if I had to date Eddie Perez."

The tomb echoed with laughter.

But Kiki didn't laugh. She stared out the window of the mausoleum, her eyes drifting over the white headstones on the hill. "Moose Morgan's buried here, isn't he?" she whispered.

Heather shivered.

Suddenly, the mausoleum was quiet. The name of Moose Morgan hung over the teenagers' heads like an invisible shroud.

Heather knew she was probably the last person to see Moose Morgan alive. He took her to Lovers' Lane that night and gave her flowers. Then he tried to force himself on her, and Heather threw his class ring into the lake. Now she wondered if she was responsible for Moose's death.

Heather tried to change the subject. "So who's the new captain of the football team?" she asked.

"You're lookin' at him," said Crusher.

Heather's eyes popped open. "You? The captain?"

Crusher leaned back against the stone wall and smiled. "Yup," he said.

Heather batted her eyes. Then she leaned back into Crusher's shoulder. "I've always wanted to date the captain of the football team, you know."

Crusher faked a yawn. "Well, if you treat me nice, Heather, maybe we can work something out."

In a matter of minutes, Heather and Crusher were locked in each other's arms, hugging and kissing.

Kiki sighed and turned back to the window.

She wanted to go home.

But Jimbo snuck up behind her—and he seemed to have other ideas on his mind. First, he put his hands on her shoulders. Then he kissed her neck.

I can't believe this, thought Kiki. I'm stuck in a graveyard with a couple of sex maniacs.

She tried to think of a way to stop Jimbo from kissing her. In desperation, she stared out the window, hoping to see a police car or something. She looked from tombstone to tombstone, seeing nothing at all . . .

But she heard something.

A sound—a scraping sound—at the edge of the cemetery.

"Hey, guys!" Kiki whispered. "Listen!"

Heather and Crusher turned their heads in mid-kiss, and Jimbo's hands froze on Kiki's shoulders. They strained to hear the wind whistling around the corners of the crypt.

"I don't hear anything," said Heather, trembling. She tried to sound tough—but she was terrified. In her mind, she saw Moose Morgan crawling out of his grave . . . calling out her name . . . reaching for her with cold, dead hands . . .

"Shhh," said Kiki. "Listen . . . there it is!"

From out of the darkness came a strange clawing sound. Like huge hands digging into wet dirt. Or fingernails scraping against wood . . .

"Someone's out there."

The creature brushed the dirt from the tops of the caskets.

At last . . .

He looked up at the violet sky from the bottom of the hole. The walls of black, moist earth seemed to close in around him and swallow him up. But it was just an illusion.

The creature had done his work well, clawing into the damp soil with his massive fingers, digging, digging, deeper and deeper. The dirt was flung up into the air with each powerful stroke of his arm—a filthy spray of mud and stones that landed in the grass and leaves around the grave. It was difficult work, and the creature's muscles burned and throbbed.

Now, he was six feet under.

The wooden caskets of his mother and father lay beneath him, two long, rotting boxes that held the secrets of his birth—the ones who spawned him, the ones who loved him . . .

At last . . .

His fingers clawed at the caskets, splinters of wood scraping away from his nails. His mind was racing, his heart bursting . . .

I'm home.

Suddenly a bolt of lightning blasted the sky over his over his head—a final gasp of the storm blowing over the mountains.

The creature felt a sudden surge of power and strength.

And then he heard something.

It came from below—an unearthly growl that shook the earth beneath him. Then he felt the two caskets shaking and vibrating against his chest.

With his arms stretched wide, the creature embraced

the caskets, as a child would hug his mother and father. He wanted to protect them—save them from whatever horror had been unleashed in the graveyard. Somehow, the creature knew that the gates of hell had been opened wide. Something was pounding, pounding its way toward him. He hugged the caskets and waited for the earth to devour him . . .

Mother . . . Father . . .

And with a sudden shock, the creature realized where the sound was coming from . . .

Inside the caskets.

No . . .

He listened in horror, his mind unable to grasp the terrible meaning of the sounds. It was too horrible to even think about. It was impossible.

But there it was again—the sound of clenched fists, pounding against the lids.

No . . .

He howled and sobbed, his brain reeling with the hideous, unspeakable truth . . .

His mother and father were buried alive.

No!!!

And they were trying to get out.

II

Home Sweet Horrible

From the diary of Sara Watkins . . .

They say that home is where the heart is. But sometimes a parent's love can devour a child's soul, like animals who eat their own young.

Victor Frankenstein created a life, then turned away in disgust. Grandfather Frank created Adam and Eve, then locked them in a cage. Adam and Eve spawned Josh and Jessie, then tried to destroy them.

These monstrous parents tried to smother their own children. But who am I to point fingers? Didn't I try to control Josh's life—even after death?

That night, as Josh sought his own gruesome homecoming in Thunder Lake Cemetery, Eddie, Jessie, and I returned home for a late dinner with our families. What a nightmare . . .

Perhaps love makes monsters of us all.

"The pot roast is dry," said Sara's mother. "It's

been sitting in the oven all night."

Sara's father looked up from his plate. "Where have you been, Sara?"

Sara picked at her food and sighed. "I'm in charge of the decorations for the Halloween Dance," she muttered. "We were working on them after school."

Her father shook his head in disbelief. "You've been making Halloween decorations for six hours? What are you building? A Frankenstein monster?"

Sara choked on her food and reached for a napkin. "Well," she said, "after the meeting, I hung out with Eddie and Jessie. We're working on a project together."

Sara's mother poured gravy over her meat and sniffed. "Isn't Eddie that Puerto Rican boy?" she asked.

Sara glared. "Yeah . . . So?"

"Do you know anything about him? I mean, his family is new in town, and, well, those people have such a different culture."

"*Those* people?" said Sara, scowling at her mother. "What do you mean by *those* people?"

Her mother wiped her mouth with a napkin and stuttered. "It's not that I'm prejudiced, Sara. It's just that, well, they're new in town. No one knows anything about them."

Sara dropped her fork on the plate. "Eddie's smart, sweet, funny, and he's a computer genius. What more do you need to know?"

Her mother shrugged. "Excuse me for worrying about you. I'm sorry." She popped a potato into her mouth and stared down at the table.

Sara's father shook his head. Then he turned to Sara and took a deep breath. It looked like he was ready to deliver a Big Speech. And he did.

"Sara," he began, "your mother and I received a letter from your teacher, Miss Nevils."

Oh, no, here it comes, thought Sara, slumping into her chair.

"It seems that your grades are slipping. Miss Nevils said you've ruined your chances for valedictorian. She also said you seem distracted . . . and that it all started when you began to associate with Eddie Perez."

Sara couldn't believe her ears.

They were blaming Eddie for her bad grades!

She opened her mouth to protest but her father interrupted. "Before you start defending yourself, Sara, your mother and I want you to know that we love you. We're not coming down on you to punish you. We just want you to share your problems with us. These last two months, we've allowed you to come and go as you please. And now we're a little worried."

Sara stared at her father, then her mother, and she didn't know what to say.

"What's going on, Sara?" her mother pleaded. "You're slipping out in the middle of the night, and you're losing sleep, too. I can tell. You seem as if you're on the edge of a nervous breakdown. What's happening to you?"

Sara looked down at the table, her eyes filled with tears. "It's Josh," she whispered. "He's so sick, I'm afraid . . . I'm afraid he's going to die." Her lie was close enough to the horrible truth that Sara couldn't stop herself from crying.

"Maybe I should take a look at him," said Sara's father, who worked as a surgeon at the county hospital.

"No," said Sara quickly. "Professor Frank has already taken him to all the specialists. They said he'll pull through . . . but, I don't know, I'm scared."

Sara's mother jumped to her feet and rushed around the table to hug Sara. She took her daughter into her arms and stroked her golden hair. "Oh, honey," she whispered. "I didn't realize Josh was so sick. Of course, you're upset. I'll call Miss Nevils and explain it all to her. Maybe she'll let you take the tests over again."

"Mother, no," said Sara.

"It's the least I can do, baby," she said, kissing Sara's forehead. "Don't you worry. Mommy and Daddy will take care of everything."

"This is the last time we're going to hold up dinner for you," said Eddie's father. "I'm starving."

Eddie sat back in his chair as his mother ladled rice and vegetables onto his plate. "I'm sorry," he said. "I lost track of the time."

Eddie's father growled into his food. "The kid can program a computer but he can't read a watch. Someday, you're going to learn the meaning of responsibility, young man."

"And someday, you're going to cut that hair," his mother added, shaking the serving spoon at him.

Eddie sighed and started to eat.

His brain was spinning. Besides the horrors of Josh

and Baskerville and the curse of Frankenstein, he was
worried about the stupid Halloween Dance. Kiki had
told him to pick her up at her house—and that meant
he needed to borrow the car.

This was not the time to ask.

"You're a strange kid, Eddie," his father grumbled.
"Most boys your age are chasing girls, not playing
with computers."

"Bite your tongue," his mother snapped at the man.
"He's too young to date girls. He's just a baby."

"With that long hair of his, the girls don't even
know he's a boy!"

Eddie rolled his eyes to the ceiling.

Now was as good a time as any.

"I have a date on Saturday night," he announced
bluntly.

His parents dropped their silverware.

"You're kidding," said his father. "With who?"

"Kiki Austin," said Eddie. "She's a cheerleader."

"My goodness!" exclaimed his mother, fanning herself with a napkin. "I think I'm going to faint. A
cheerleader?"

Eddie nodded.

His father grinned and slapped him on the back.
"Thatta boy!" Then he turned to his wife. "I told you
he had it in him!"

Eddie cleared his throat. "There's just one thing,"
he said quietly. "I need to borrow the car."

His parents froze.

"You?" said his father slowly. "Mr. Responsibility?
You want to borrow the car? I don't know."

Eddie sighed.

His mother reached for her husband's arm and squeezed. "But, Julio," she said, "it's his first date!"

"I know it's his first date! But it's my new convertible! What if he smashes it up? We're not insured for that!"

"Julio, please . . ."

Eddie's father stared down at his food, then looked his son in the eye. "All right, Eddie," he said, pointing his fork at the boy's throat. "But if you get one scratch . . . one scratch . . . on my new convertible . . ."

Eddie held his breath and glared at his father.

"I don't care if you *are* my only son, I'll kill you if you wreck my car. You got that, Mr. Responsibility?"

"Yes, Dad."

Jessie and Grandfather Frank sat in the dining room of the Frank family mansion, sipping their soup in silence.

"Josh is quiet tonight, isn't he?" said Grandfather Frank.

"Yeah," said Jessie. "Usually, he's howling for food now. Maybe he fell asleep. I'll feed him as soon as I finish this soup."

The old man nodded.

Jessie's stomach was doing somersaults—not because of the soup. She was nervous about asking her grandfather the Big Question. She swallowed a spoonful of soup and gathered up her courage.

"Can I go on a date Saturday night?"

Grandfather Frank's head snapped up, his eyes blazing. "A date?" he said.

"Yeah," Jessie said quickly. "It's just the Halloween Dance at school, it's not like a real date. There'll be lots of people there, including teachers, it's only a dance."

"Jessie!" the old man interrupted. "I can't believe you'd entertain such a thought . . . after everything that's happened!"

Jessie sighed. "What do you mean?"

Grandfather Frank stood up and paced the length of the old dining room. "You know that Josh's blood turned bad before he died. And you know the same thing could happen to you!"

"But I'm fine right now!" Jessie pleaded. "Josh didn't turn into a monster overnight! What are you so worried about?"

Grandfather Frank stopped in front of her. "This isn't a game, Jessie! It's a matter of life and death!"

"What are you talking about!"

The old man slammed his fist on the table. "Don't you understand? I can't let you mingle with boys! What if this tainted blood is passed on to another generation?"

Jessie jumped up from her chair. "I'm just going to the dance with him! I'm not planning to *mate* with him! I can't believe you'd think that about me!"

A cold silence fell over the room.

Grandfather Frank lowered his head in shame. "You're right. Forgive me, Jessie," he said. "I'm so upset about the tragic results of my experiments. I only want to avoid further complications."

"Well, don't worry," said Jessie. "I'm not planning to populate the world with Frankenstein's children. I just want to put on a scary costume and dance around and have a little fun . . . just this one night. I need it, Grandfather. I need to get away from this . . . this nightmare . . . even if it's only for a few hours."

Grandfather Frank returned to his seat. "You're absolutely right, my child. I suppose all of us have been a little jumpy lately. I'm sorry if I snapped at you."

"No problem," said Jessie, sitting down at the table.

Grandfather looked up from his soup and smiled. "So who is the lucky gentleman?"

Jessie's heart stopped. "Well . . . aah . . . he's a really nice guy. A freshman in my class, with a great sense of humor . . . You'd like him."

"And what's his name?"

"Mike Morgan."

The soup spoon paused before Grandfather Frank's lips. "Any relation to Moose Morgan?" he asked.

Jessie squirmed in her seat. "He's Moose's little brother."

Grandfather Frank sipped from his spoon and shook his head. "I'm not going to say a word, Jessie. I just hope you know what you're doing."

"Me, too," she muttered.

A terrible silence filled the mansion. No growling in the basement. No bars rattling in the cage. It was eerie.

"I guess I'll feed Josh now," said Jessie, getting up from the table. "It's strange how quiet he is tonight."

"Very strange," the old man agreed.

And then Jessie walked to the kitchen and prepared a meal for her brother—a bowl of soup, half a loaf of bread, and a banana. She balanced the tray of food with one hand as she climbed down the basement stairs. But it wasn't until she turned on the lights that she discovered Josh's cage was empty.

Her first impulse was to scream. Which she did.

Her second impulse was to call Sara and Eddie. Which she also did.

And her third impulse was to try to figure out where Josh might have gone. Of course, she never guessed the truth—that at this very moment, Josh was having a family reunion in a graveyard . . .

With their dead mother and father.

12

❖❖❖❖❖❖❖❖❖❖❖❖❖❖❖❖❖❖❖❖❖❖❖❖❖

Family Reunion

From a song by Joshua Frank, written two years before
his death . . .

> I wish I remembered their faces,
> Their voices, their smiles, their eyes.
> But time takes away all reminders.
> Once buried, a memory dies.

> I wish I remembered my mother.
> Her kisses still burn on my cheek.
> I wish I remembered my father.
> His love is the phantom I seek.

> But death shows no mercy for children.
> The funeral bells must toll,
> And the things buried six feet under
> Are like worms that feed on my soul.

> The preacher said someday I'll join them.

Until then, they'll watch over me.
But will I remember their faces?
And what if I fear what I see?

A scourge of wind blasted the cemetery throughout. Dead autumn leaves danced and swirled in the air, mocking the naked graves below. The clawlike branch of a tree swayed, then scraped the rooftop of a hollow crypt like a skeletal hand beating a drum. Then, with a high-pitched scream, the wind plummeted down the hill, through the trees, across the lake . . .

And the boneyard was silent.

Huddled together in the open window of a mausoleum, four teenagers gazed out into the night.

"I don't see anything," said Heather Leigh Clark. "Just a bunch of tombstones."

"Shhh," said Kiki. "Listen."

Jimbo and Crusher leaned out the window, their hands clutching the girls' shoulders for balance. They tilted their heads, listened . . .

And there it was.

A scraping sound at the bottom of the hill.

It sent chills up their spines—a cold, eerie sensation that made their pulses race. But Jimbo and Crusher were tough guys—high school football stars—and they'd never admit to being afraid.

"Let's go check it out," said Crusher.

"Yeah," Jimbo agreed.

"What?" said Kiki. "I'm not going down there! Are you crazy? I just want to go home."

"Look," said Crusher. "It's probably some other

crypt-kickers lookin' for fun. We'll go scare 'em. You girls stay here."

"No way," said Heather. "That's how it always happens in the horror movies. The guys leave the girls alone, and the girls get attacked by zombies. If you're going out there, so are we."

"We are?" said Kiki, trembling.

"Yeah, come on."

One by one, they crawled out of the mausoleum window, landing with a soft squish onto a wet bed of leaves. Then the guys took the lead, and the four teenagers began walking down the graveyard hill. Halfway down, Kiki tripped over a small headstone. At first, she thought it was a zombie reaching up from the grave—then she laughed at herself for being so clumsy.

Heather—who was trying hard to act brave—was suddenly filled with terror. Because she realized what was buried at the bottom of the hill . . .

Moose Morgan's corpse.

Maybe he's mad at me, she thought to herself. Maybe he wants revenge for the way I treated him on Lovers' Lane.

She began to wonder what his body would look like, after being buried for a few days. Would his corpse be rotted? Decayed? Crawling with worms?

Stop it, Heather, she told herself. Get a grip.

Then she heard a low growl rise up from the bottom of the hill—and it sounded like it came from beneath the earth.

The four teenagers froze.

Jimbo grabbed Crusher's arm. "Did you hear that?"

he whispered. "Something's inside that grave down there."

Kiki and Heather rushed up behind the boys. "What do you think it is?" Heather gasped.

Then another sound rose up from the grave—a sound that made their blood run cold.

It was the sound of someone crying.

The creature sobbed and clawed the casket lids—until blue streams of blood flowed from his fingernails.

The pounding was louder now. The things inside the caskets were using all their strength to escape.

Mother . . . Father . . .

The creature howled in anguish. And a crash of distant thunder echoed his cry. The earth itself seemed to pulse and vibrate beneath him. The wooden planks of the caskets buckled and cracked . . .

And the lids burst open.

A blast of foul air erupted from the broken boxes—a vile, infernal smell of death, decay, and hell itself. Then came the screaming—bellowing roars of unearthly rage and emotion.

The creature howled.

And two pairs of rotted hands reached up from inside the caskets—and embraced him.

Their heads burst through the wood, two grinning skulls barely covered with flesh. Their faces were alive with hungry worms that burrowed and feasted on their cheeks. Their hair was wild and long and speckled with white maggots. And clusters of steel wires sparked and hissed from their necks like a nest of poisonous vipers.

Yes, the creature howled—but not from fear.

He was happy, ecstatic, as these two hideous beings wrapped their rotted arms around him. They were the ones who loved him, the ones who cared . . .

His mother and his father.

And they knew who he was. They pulled their decaying bodies up out of the caskets, their sunken eyes filled with tears, and they hugged him and held him and stroked his black flowing hair.

At last . . .

Josh had come home.

For a moment all was silent in this black hole in the earth—as the long-buried creatures embraced their only son. They growled softly in his ear and wept cold, bitter tears.

Josh looked deep into his mother's eyes. The cold dark orbs reminded him of his sister. And his father's eyes made him feel as if he were looking into a mirror.

Mother . . . Father . . .

They stared at the creature—their son—hardly believing what they were seeing.

Then they reached out with gray, bony fingers and touched the steel bolts in Josh's neck . . . the scars and stitches that covered Josh's face . . . the artificial joints of his long, grotesque limbs . . .

And they howled in fury.

Their unearthly roars rose up, in unison, from the depths of the grave—and echoed throughout the cemetery.

They understood . . .

Their son had been cheated from death. Their son had been cursed with life everlasting. Their son was a monster . . .

Just like his mother and father.

Josh reached out for the parents he hardly knew. His eyes were wet with tears, his vision blurred. But still, in the gloom of the grave, he could see just how horrible, how cruel and unkind, fate had been to his parents.

They were hideous, ugly things.

But they were the only things that loved him.

A sudden wave of emotion swept through the boy— a powerful sense of joy and belonging that drove him to his feet, up and out of the grave, howling and roaring . . .

And when he rose above the earth, he felt a painful jolt in his stomach—and was tackled to the ground . . .

By Jimbo and Crusher.

Heather Leigh Clark screamed and dropped down behind a gravestone.

It's Moose, she told herself. It's the corpse of Moose Morgan . . . and he's coming to get me!

Kiki Austin stood beside her in shock, unable to move. She couldn't believe her eyes.

It looked like a monster had jumped out of the grave, and Jimbo and Crusher had tackled it!

She watched in horror as the two football players rolled around in the wet leaves and grass, trying to pin the giant creature against a flat marble stone. The creature roared like a wild beast. Its cry was so lonely, so anguished, Kiki almost felt sorry for the poor thing.

Then something happened that sent Kiki's mind over the edge . . .

Two half-rotted corpses crawled out of the open grave—and attacked Jimbo and Crusher. One of them was a woman with wild, white-streaked hair. As the she-creature grabbed Jimbo's neck with her skeletal claws, the taller corpse went after Crusher. He picked up the huge football player with both hands and hurled him into the air. Crusher screamed as he slammed against a gravestone, knocking it to the ground.

Jimbo was trying to yell for help, but the she-beast choked off his cries and swung him around. Jimbo kicked his feet madly, tipping over tombstones as he spun through the air.

Kiki looked down at Heather Leigh Clark, trembling behind a gravestone. She had never seen the blond cheerleader look so frightened, so out of control . . .

"No, Moose, no," Heather wept, clinging to the stone. "I'm sorry, Moose, don't hurt me . . ."

Kiki reached down to touch Heather's shoulder. Heather's eyes popped open, her face inches away from the marble engraving on the tombstone . . .

It was Moose Morgan's grave.

"Nooooo!"

Heather screamed at the top of her lungs and staggered backward, knocking Kiki over as she tried to crawl away. "No, Moose, no!" she gasped hysterically, sobbing and screaming uncontrollably.

Kiki pulled herself off the ground and looked down

toward the open grave . . .

The three monsters were staring at them.

"Run, Heather! Run!"

Kiki tried to pull Heather to her feet. But it was too late. The she-corpse was on top of them both, digging her long fingernails into their hair and pulling them backward.

"My hair!" Heather shrieked. "Don't touch my hair!"

She reached around to grab hold of the creature's wrist. And she screamed in terror when flakes of skin pulled away in her hands.

Twenty feet away, Crusher was slowly regaining consciousness. For a moment, he didn't know where he was. Then he saw the gravestone lying on the ground. And then he heard Kiki and Heather screaming.

Jumping to his feet, the huge football player charged at the she-beast and threw himself on top of her. She screeched as she fell, her hand pulling a blond lock of hair out of Heather's head.

"Ouch!!!" the girl shouted. "That hurt!"

The two male monsters rushed to help the mother as she thrashed beneath Crusher's weight. Together, they pulled the boy off of her and threw him against a marble statue that toppled to the ground.

Jimbo was on his feet now. He grabbed Crusher, pulled him up, and shouted, "Let's get out of here!"

Then the four teenagers ran for their lives, their hearts pounding as they headed for the gates of Thunder Lake Cemetery. Kiki and Heather couldn't run as fast as the boys. But Jimbo and Crusher didn't care.

They just wanted to get out—alive.

Suddenly, as they approached the gates, a blinding light flashed in their eyes—and a booming voice echoed in the night . . .

"Freeze! This is Officer Colker! You kids are under arrest!"

On the edge of the cemetery, Josh watched his parents break through the iron fence and disappear into the woods.

Where were they going?

He ducked through the bars and followed them. The woods were dark and silent. Not a creature was stirring. Then he heard a branch snap, and he turned his head. There they were, trying to push through a wall of thorny bushes.

Josh raised his hand and grunted.

His mother and father stopped. They turned their grotesque heads slowly, their eyes burning like coals. And they waited for their son to catch up.

As Josh staggered through the woods toward them, he wished he could say something to them . . .

Tell them about his sorrow and his pain. Tell them that he loved them.

But how could he ever find the words?

His brain was so muddled—shattered and patched together like a broken vase that could never hold water again. He was damaged and mute . . .

But they, too, seemed incapable of speech.

Maybe they could communicate with their hearts. Maybe love could say it all.

His mother and father stood together in the darkness, the thorns piercing their flesh. Their gray, rotting faces twisted and turned, and the black, parched lips pulled away from their teeth. They were smiling at him—smiling and holding out their hands.

Josh felt the tears coming to his eyes again.

Yes, they loved him.

Love . . .

And as he stepped into their arms, feeling the cold comfort of the grave wrap around him, Josh's heart was bursting with emotion. He rested his giant head on his mother's shoulder and cried like a baby—cried for the parents he lost, the life he left behind, and the girl that he loved . . .

Sara . . .

He knew this was all he could ever hope for, love and understanding in the arms of his parents. Everything else was lost forever. There was only one other thing he wanted . . .

Revenge.

Revenge for being the son of monsters. Revenge for being resurrected. Revenge for being the living subject of a madman's experiments.

Grandfather Frank.

How could Josh tell his mother and father? How could he let them know who did this to him?

He pulled away from his mother's embrace and pointed at the steel knobs in his necks . . . the stitches and scars . . . the hideous limbs . . .

Then he looked into their eyes. His mother turned to his father and nodded. Their eyes were glowing—with understanding, with anger and rage. The father raised his fist to the heavens and shook it. The mother tilted back her head and screeched.

Yes, they understood.

Because Grandfather Frank had created them, too.

Then the two zombies turned away from their son and stepped deeper into the thorns. Josh saw the fierce gleam in their eyes as they stalked away—and heard the terrible fury rising from their rotted throats . . .

Somehow, it frightened him.

His mother and father were about to unleash all the rage that had been buried in Thunder Lake Cemetery for almost twelve years.

They were planning to avenge the Frankenstein curse once and for all.

And they'd kill anyone who got in their way.

13

Tales From the Crypt

From *The Coal County Daily News* . . .

CEMETERY VANDALS ARRESTED
Accused Teens Blame "Zombies"

From *The Weekly Thunder* . . .

CRYPT-KICKERS DENY CHARGES
"It was Moose Morgan's corpse!"
claims cheerleader

From *The Pennsylvania Scandal* . . .

GRAVEYARD ZOMBIE MASSACRE!
Elvis Sighted Among the Dead

Sara attached the wires to the electrodes and covered the body with a white sheet.

She couldn't believe the Halloween Dance committee had chosen "Frankenstein" as their theme this year. And she couldn't believe *she* had to decorate it. It was too weird.

There she was—in the middle of the gymnasium with a half-dozen volunteers—reconstructing the gruesome experiment that had turned her life into a nightmare. If only they knew . . .

"Sara," said Mike Morgan, holding a bunch of cardboard cutouts covered in aluminum foil. "Where should I hang these lightning bolts?"

Sara looked up to the ceiling. A fake electrical tower hung down from the middle of the gym—mock gothic machinery made of cardboard and wire and foam balls spray-painted silver. Suspended in the air was a row of Victorian window frames, and behind them, a wall of puffy gray clouds and foiled lightning bolts.

"We already have enough lightning in the sky," Sara said to Mike. "But we need more in the center, over the galvanizer. Hang them all around it and place a few bolts over the corpse, too."

Mike Morgan grinned. "Sure thing, Professor," he said. "You seem to be an expert at this."

Sara shrugged. "I guess I'm a mad scientist at heart."

Mike laughed and went to get the ladder. Sara watched him walk away—and felt a terrible pang of guilt. He was such a nice kid, the perfect boy for Jessie. If only Josh hadn't killed Mike's brother.

If only . . .

Sara felt a sudden mist of tears come to her eyes. She looked down at the stuffed dummy on the lab

table—and remembered the night Josh killed himself.
Grandfather Frank had placed his body on the dining-
room table, beneath a white sheet. And that's when
the nightmare began.

She looked around the gymnasium—at the cardboard fantasy world that mocked her horrible experi
ments. One wall of the gym was set up to look
like a morgue, with fake human parts sticking out
of brown-paper file cabinets. Sara had written the
names of schoolteachers on the drawers as a joke—
but she couldn't laugh about it, for very good reason.
She had seen the inside of a morgue. And she had
stolen body parts, too. The sound of the bone saw
still seemed to ring in her ear.

Mike Morgan dragged the tallest ladder toward her.
"How about that lab table. Sara?" he asked. "Want me
to suspend it under the galvanizer?"

Sara cleared her throat. "If you can manage it," she
said. "It's pretty heavy."

"No problem."

"Thanks, Mike." She smiled. "I'm going to check
out the graveyard and see how Kiki's doing."

Then she turned and walked toward the exit of the
gym. Her eyes took in the ghoulish details of the decorations—the anatomy posters, the skeletons, the jars of
fake eyeballs and brains and hearts. She shuddered as
she walked, all too aware of the reality behind the
horror movie fantasy. If only they knew . . .

Frankenstein was real.

She stepped into the hallway outside the gym—
and entered a cardboard graveyard that was chillingly
authentic.

"Kiki," she said. "You're doing a wonderful job. It looks so real."

The redheaded cheerleader looked up from the open casket she had arranged beneath a tombstone. She smiled. "Thanks, Sara. I guess my big adventure in the cemetery last night inspired me."

Sara's stomach clenched up in a knot. She had heard all the stories—some said Moose Morgan had crawled out of the grave and attacked some football players. Others said there was a whole army of walking dead. Of course, Sara didn't believe it. But one horrible fact couldn't be denied . . .

Josh had escaped from his cage.

"Do you need some help?" she asked Kiki.

"Oh, sure. Could you spread those cobwebs over the headstones? Make it look real creepy-crawly, you know?"

Sara crouched down and plucked a strand of cottony cobweb material, then stretched it across the cardboard crypt. She was dying to ask Kiki a few questions. She had to know the truth.

"Kiki?"

"Yeah?"

"What really happened in the graveyard last night?"

Kiki closed her eyes and gasped. "You wouldn't believe it if I told you, Sara. The cops think we're crazy. But when they saw all the damage . . . and that open grave . . ."

"Open grave?" Sara's heart began to race.

"Yup," said Kiki, brushing her hair out of her eyes. "Here's what happened. Me and Heather went to the cemetery with Jimbo and Crusher, just to party, you

know? We went inside this big mausoleum on the
hill, and everything was quiet and, well, you know.
Anyway, I hear this funny sound coming from the
edge of the cemetery. It sounded like growling . . .
or crying, maybe. Then we heard scraping."

"Scraping?"

"Yeah. Like fingernails on a casket. We climbed
out of the crypt to go take a look. At the bottom of
the hill, we saw this big open grave. And there was
something inside, making noises. Jimbo and Crusher tiptoed up to take a look. And this big monster
jumped out!"

"A monster?"

"Yeah, covered with stitches and scars and bandages and stuff. He had a big ugly head, and big arms
and legs. And, oh, yeah, he had these metal knobs in
his neck."

Sara knew instantly who she was talking about . . .
Josh . . .

Her heart skipped a beat. She was afraid to ask
what happened next.

"When this monster jumped out of the grave, Jimbo
and Crusher tackled him. You know, like a football tackle. They had him pinned down against a
headstone . . . and that's when it got really freaky.
I'm gonna have nightmares for the rest of my life,
I'm sure."

"What happened?" Sara had to know.

"Get this. The monster's yelling and kicking. And
then these two zombies crawl out of the grave!"

"Zombies?"

"Yeah," said Kiki. "A man and a woman zombie! They looked just like the monster, but older, you know? More rotted and ugly . . . like they'd been buried a long time. And they had worms crawling on their faces . . . and wires sticking out of their necks."

"Wires?"

Sara's mind was reeling. Kiki's description was too accurate to be a hallucination. A man and a woman zombie? With wires in their necks? It couldn't be true. Or could it? Sara had a slow sinking feeling that she knew who they were . . .

Josh's mother and father.

And they'd risen from the grave.

"Heather keeps telling everyone it was the corpse of Moose Morgan. But she was so scared, she had her eyes shut the whole time," said Kiki, erecting another cardboard grave. "I saw everything. And I don't care if the cops don't believe me. They know we didn't dig up that grave and tear up the caskets. We didn't have any shovels. But they don't want to believe the truth. There were three monsters . . . a boy monster, a mommy monster, and a daddy monster. And no one believes me."

"I believe you," Sara muttered under her breath.

She looked up to see Eddie and Jessie walking down the hall. They smiled grimly and waved. Sara motioned to them with her head, pointing toward the gym. "I'm going back inside," she said to Kiki. "There's still a lot to do." Then she slipped away and met Jessie and Eddie near the make-believe morgue.

"Any luck?" she asked them.

Eddie shook his head. "No," he sighed. "I wasted my whole lunch hour riding around on my bike."

"Me, too," said Jessie. "No sign of him anywhere."

Sara glanced around her, making sure no one could hear. "Listen," she whispered. "We have another problem. Josh isn't the only monster on the loose."

"What are you talking about?" said Jessie.

Sara looked into Jessie's eyes. How could she tell her the awful news—that her parents were still alive? She took a deep breath and spoke . . .

"Josh went to the cemetery last night and dug up your parents' grave."

Jessie's jaw dropped.

"It gets weirder," said Sara, pausing. "It seems that they're still alive. They climbed out of the grave and attacked Jimbo and Crusher. Kiki Austin saw it all."

"Kiki?" said Eddie, wide-eyed. "My date for the dance?"

"Do you know any other Kikis?" said Jessie impatiently. "What about my parents? Tell me everything!"

Sara sighed. "I don't know much more."

"Well, how did they come to life?"

Sara shuddered. "I hate to say it, Jessie. But I suspect they were buried alive."

Jessie trembled. The horror of being sealed in a tomb—for almost twelve years—was too ghastly to imagine. "What did they look like?" she asked, afraid to hear the answer.

Sara took a deep breath. "Kiki said they were ugly and rotted and covered with worms. She called them monsters."

Jessie looked down at the floor. "Just what my family needs," she muttered. "More monsters."

When Jessie looked up at Sara, her eyes were filled with tears. Sara understood her pain and anguish. It was terrible news—a nightmare that refused to die. She put her arm around Jessie's shoulder as she began to cry.

"I can't believe it," the young girl wept. "My brother's a monster, my parents are zombies, and I'm doomed to follow in their footsteps. I'm cursed. We're all cursed."

Sara hugged her. "It's going to be okay," she whispered. "I'm not going to let anything happen to you, Jessie. I love you. You're the greatest."

Jessie smiled and brushed away her tears. "If I'm so great, why am I crying in the middle of the gym?"

"Jessie! Yo!"

She looked up to see Mike Morgan, perched high on the ladder with an aluminum foil lightning bolt in his hand. He grinned and waved.

"Hi, Mike!"

Jessie waved back, smiling through her tears. Then she looked at Eddie and Sara, and shrugged. "There's only one thing I can say," she whispered.

Eddie and Sara looked at her.

"This is going to be one helluva scary Halloween."

14

The Night Before Halloween

From the diary of Sara Watkins . . .

Love is the phantom that haunts every human heart.
Its shape and substance cannot be defined, but its
power is undeniable—and frightening. It was love
that brought Josh and me together when the world
seemed dark. It was love that compelled me to defy
nature and bring him back to life. And it was love
that beckoned this cursed creature to Thunder Lake
Cemetery where buried passions refused to die . . .
Now, on the eve of Halloween, the world is haunted
by things that should be dead. But sometimes I wonder
if it's the other way around. Perhaps it is the dead
who are haunted . . .
By the love of all who live.

'Twas the night before Halloween, and all through
the town, not a creature was stirring—except every kid

who waited until the last minute to make a Halloween costume.

Eddie was one of the lucky ones. His mother was so thrilled about his first date, she threw herself—body and soul—into the creation of a magnificent outfit. As she slaved over the sewing machine, cursing under her breath, Eddie locked himself in his bedroom.

"Let's see now," he muttered to himself. "Reverse the negative and positive charges and . . . what are they talking about?"

He stared at the electronics textbook and scratched his head. Then he held a magnifying glass over the remote control unit of the TV set. The parts were so small it was hard to see what went where . . .

There it was.

With a pair of tweezers, he disconnected the tiny wires.

If this works, he thought, those monsters'll be no problem. I'll just change the channel.

He was trying to create a sort of "stun gun" that would work on reanimated flesh—an electrical charge that would scramble their own internal current. He had no idea if the thing would work . . .

But with *three* monsters on the loose, it was certainly worth a try.

Suddenly there was a knock at the door.

"Eddie, honey, it's me."

His mother.

"I'm busy, Mom."

Another knock. "Let me in. I need to hem the cape, and I want to make sure the length is right."

Eddie sighed and pulled himself away from his work. He unlocked the door, and his mother pushed through, holding up a long vampire cape.

Eddie gasped when he saw it—he couldn't help himself. "Mom, it's beautiful. Really. I'm impressed."

His mother beamed and held it up. The flowing black cape was lined with red satin, and the collar flared out like the wings of a vampire bat. It was remarkably authentic—Dracula himself would approve.

"Turn around, try it on," his mother ordered. "Let's see how the collar looks. That's it. Perfect! It'll look great with your father's suit, the one he wore to Aunt Carlita's funeral. And I even have a star pendant you can wear."

Eddie didn't know what to say. He was overwhelmed by his mother's enthusiasm.

"So, spin around, Count Dracula," she said. "Take a look in the mirror."

Eddie turned and stared in the mirror. Not bad. Sort of dashing. He clutched the sides of the cape and raised his right arm. The rich fabric swooped through the air like a creature of the night. Then he covered his face, vampire style, and arched his eyebrows.

"You scare me, you look so sinister," his mother cried, clapping her hands together. "And very handsome, too."

Eddie studied his face in the mirror—and to his own surprise, he had to admit she was right.

He *did* look kind of handsome.

"Now, don't move, Eddie," said his mother. "I need to pin the hem, then I can finish it."

She knelt on the floor with a few pins in her mouth and began to adjust the hem of the cape. Out of the corner of her eye, she saw the stuff on his desk.

"What's that?" she asked. "The remote control?"

"Yeah," Eddie stuttered. "I'm, ah, taking it apart for a school project. Don't worry, I'll put it back together again."

"I hope so," said his mother. "Heaven forbid your father has to get up off the couch. If you break it, he'll kill you."

"Well, he hasn't killed me yet."

"Don't push your luck," she said, standing up. "All finished. Take it off. I've got work to do."

"Me, too," said Eddie, returning to his desk. His mother closed the door behind her, and Eddie tried to finish the adjustments on the remote control.

Finally, it was ready.

He turned on his radio and increased the volume of the music. Then he pointed the remote control at the radio and pushed the pause button. The radio went dead . . .

Victory.

Now I just need to hunt down those monsters, he thought. But where?

He thought about Josh—his love of music, his guitar, his family, his home. And he tried to think of the one thing in the world that Josh loved most of all . . .

Sara.

That's it, Eddie thought. Sooner or later, he's going to look for Sara. He loves her . . . as much as I do. He'll come for her, in the night.

And I'll be waiting there for him.

Sara Watkins stared at herself in the mirror—and tried not to scream.

At first, she thought her costume was a great idea, a stroke of genius. She'd show everyone she had a sense of humor. At school, they called her the Ice Witch behind her back—because she seemed so studious and reserved. What could be more ingenious than to dress up as . . . a real Ice Witch!

But now, seeing herself in the mirror, she had some doubts.

She wore her mother's white formal gown, a long, strapless dress with cold, sleek lines. Her blond hair was pulled back in a severe bun and tucked into a tall witch's hat that she spray-painted white and adorned with plastic icicles. Her face was powdered to a pale gleam, her eyes streaked with harsh blue shadows.

She *was* the Ice Witch.

Sara stared in shocked silence at her own face, hardly believing what she saw. It was a cold face, a bitter face, hardened by pain and sorrow—a face without pity, without warmth, without emotion . . .

Is that how they see me? she wondered. Or is that how I really am?

She thought about Josh—and began to question her own ability to love. After he escaped from his cage, he must have been so frightened, so alone, so desperate for affection. But he went to the graveyard seeking comfort—not to the girl he once loved . . .

Sara looked in the mirror again. Her face was streaked with tears, the makeup running down her face like jagged bolts of blue lightning.

Josh . . .

"I love you," she whispered. "I love you, I love you, I love you . . ."

And she fell to her knees on the floor, sobbing and glaring at her own chilling reflection.

"What good is the love of an Ice Witch?" she wept. "It's cold and it's cruel, and it freezes everything it touches."

Her mind replayed the horror of Josh's suicide—and her own heartless response. She dissected his body, rearranged and rebuilt it, with cold scientific precision. Then she locked him in a cage, studied him like an animal, and trembled in fear when he reached out for her . . .

"The love of an Ice Witch is a love that never lasts," she said, choking on her tears. "If you try to hold it in your hands, it melts . . ."

Sara hugged her knees and cried, her heart aching with empty feelings of loss and self-doubt. She didn't know who she was anymore. She didn't know who she loved—or if she was even capable of love. But the most painful thought of all was . . .

Could anyone ever really love her—without getting hurt?

She reached up and touched the mirror with her hand. Then she scraped her fingernails across her own reflection, clawing at the image like a cat, scratching and slashing her own worst enemy. The sound of her nails against glass was sharp and cold . . .

And it was echoed by a scratching sound at her bedroom window.

Sara gasped and turned her head. There was someone at her window, clawing at the glass. Slowly she stood up and took one step forward.

There, silhouetted by streetlights, was a tall, unearthly figure, its head horribly inhuman, its massive shoulders wider than the window . . .

It was Josh.

Sara rushed forward with tears in her eyes.

He had come for her.

She flung open the window, and the creature took a step backward, into the shadows. His eyes were blazing in the darkness. She whispered his name. And he answered her, in that sad, cracked voice . . .

"Sa . . . ra."

She reached out her hands to him, wanting to touch him, hold him, feel him. But the bandaged creature stayed low to the ground—a macabre, lovestruck Romeo gazing at his Juliet . . .

He took another step backward, his hand held out before him. He was beckoning her, calling her out into the night. He looked like a phantom, standing there in the shadows of her front yard. Like the phantom of love that had eluded Sara all of her life . . .

She had to go to him, follow him wherever he went.

And as she slipped into jeans and a sweatshirt, she suddenly realized where Josh was going to take her . . .

To meet his parents.

Jessie couldn't believe she was going out to the old mill. By herself. At night.

But Mike Morgan had his heart set on being King Tut for Halloween—and Jessie agreed to be Queen Nefertiti. Mike was so excited about it, he even made two headpieces out of papier-mâché. And Jessie—like a fool—told him she could supply *oodles* of bandages . . .

Unfortunately, all the bandages were inside the mill.

And the mill was the last place Jessie wanted to go on the night before Halloween—after her mom and dad had crawled out of the grave.

But she had made a promise. And now she was racing along the edge of the lake as fast as she could, heading for the place of Josh's resurrection. The mill . . .

She could hear Baskerville sniffing at the door while she fumbled with the lock. She pushed it open—and the huge black hound jumped up on her shoulders, licking her face and panting with delight.

"Baskerville, baby! How are you, my sweet, precious Frankenpooch!"

She snapped on the lights and noticed that, once again, the reanimated beast hadn't touched his dog food. She looked down at Baskerville. Besides the electrodes in his neck, he was the picture of health—dog health, anyway.

"There must be a lot of mice in here, Baskerbaby," she said. "Or else you'd be skin and bones. How can you eat all those cute little mice?"

Baskerville barked and wagged his tail.

"I might as well get this over with," she said to herself, walking toward the corner cabinet with her backpack. She opened a drawer full of bandages and emptied it into her bag. Baskerville danced around her feet, happy to see her.

Then a strange thing happened.

The huge dog pricked up his ears and snapped his head around toward the door. Jessie could see the sleek black hair rising on his back. He heard something outside . . .

And then he started to growl.

Jessie slowly zipped up her backpack and slipped it over her shoulders. Her heart was pounding in her chest. She could feel the electricity in the air—an invisible current flowing from the dog at her feet . . . and whatever was outside the door.

She reached down and grabbed Baskerville's leash. Then she moved slowly, step by step, toward the door. The closer she got, the more intense her fear.

"You'll protect me, won't you, Baskerville?" she whispered, stepping into the doorway.

Baskerville growled as Jessie peered into the darkness. At first, she saw nothing. Then she heard the sound of breathing, about ten feet in front of her . . .

"Who's out there?" she said in a firm voice. "Josh? Is that you? Who's out there?"

Two shadows stirred in the darkness—then stepped into the light . . .

Jessie tried to scream, but she couldn't. She was petrified—spellbound—by the sight of two hideous creatures standing before her. They were the most horrible things she had ever seen, worse than any late-night zombie movie on TV. Because they were real.

The man was nearly seven feet tall, with a wide skeletal frame and gaunt limbs that hung by his sides.

His flesh was gray and thin and rotted, and his face was thin and drawn, like Josh's, but crawling with worms. The woman was almost as tall as her husband and even thinner. A cluster of wires burst through the decayed flesh of her throat, and her wild mane of hair seemed to twist and writhe like a living thing in pain. With horror, Jessie realized the hair was filled with thousands of tiny white maggots . . .

Her first impulse was to scream and run. But her second impulse was much more complex—a witch's brew of emotions, spiced with curiosity, fascination, and childlike wonder.

She had never seen her mother and father before.

Without warning, Baskerville unleashed a loud, ferocious howl . . .

And he lunged at the creatures.

Jessie pulled hard on the leash, but stumbled forward into the night. "Baskerville! No!"

It was too late. The giant dog barked and snapped—and frightened the creatures away. Jessie watched them shamble off, two unearthly shadows in the woods by the lake. Suddenly she realized that she wasn't afraid anymore. Her heart was filled with a strange empty longing—a desire that had burned deep within her as long as she could remember . . .

To be reunited with her mother and father.

"I'm going to follow them," she said in a clear, determined voice. She gripped the dog's leash as tight as she could. "And you're coming along, too, Baskerville."

'Twas the night before Halloween, and all through the town, not a creature was stirring—except Eddie Perez, who hid behind bushes, watching Sara from a distance as she followed her resurrected boyfriend. And Jessie, who crept through the woods with her reanimated dog, trailing two bone-thin creatures that had crawled from the grave. And all of them—the cursed and the damned—were heading straight for the same godforsaken place . . .

A house of forbidden dreams and nightmares everlasting.

The House of Frankenstein.

15

When Nightmares Come Home

From the secret journal of Professor Frank . . .

The creature named Josh has escaped from his cage. But instead of remorse, I feel only relief. He was the last in a long line of failures—as savage a brute as the original Frankenstein monster.

I suppose I shouldn't have enlisted Sara and Jessie in the grim task of resurrecting my "grandson." I used them—like artificial hands—to achieve my own scientific desires. But the experiment should have worked this time! It should have succeeded!

Ah, but the mysteries of life and death still elude me. A living nightmare has been unleashed upon the world. And I fear, when that nightmare comes home . . .

There'll be hell to pay.

Grandfather Frank looked up from his journal.

He thought he heard something. A groan. Outside. But as he listened more carefully, he decided it was just the wind blowing through the ancient rafters of the Frank family mansion. He gazed with a bitter smile at the volumes of books that filled his library—and wondered how a man of science could allow himself to be frightened by the wind . . .

Old fool, he thought to himself. You've robbed morgues and disturbed fresh graves, yet you fear the dark like a child.

He shrugged his shoulders and picked up his pen, trying to write another line in his precious secret journal. But for some reason, he couldn't collect his thoughts. It wasn't too hard to figure out why . . .

Josh.

He was out there, lurking in the darkness, plotting his revenge. Grandfather Frank remembered the threat in Josh's final message . . .

If you dare to resurrect me from the dead, I promise you this—I'll hunt you down and kill you if it's the last thing I do.

The old man shuddered and stared uneasily through the library window. Then he got up from his desk, walked across the room, and closed the thick velvet drapes.

I'll show you just how monstrous I really am.

Josh's words echoed in his mind, louder and louder, until the old man clamped his gnarled hands over his ears, trying to block out the voice of vengeance . . .

Resurrect me—and die.

Teetering on the brink of madness, Grandfather Frank spun around with a single sudden jolt . . .

Because someone was knocking on the front door. No, not knocking—pounding—like an earthquake or tidal wave, a devastating force of nature that shook the whole mansion like a fragile house of cards. For a single terrifying moment, Grandfather Frank imagined the walls tumbling down on top of him—burying him alive with his journals, his books . . . and the very secret of life itself.

The thought of being buried alive was so horrifying to Grandfather Frank, his mind nearly snapped.

But then another booming knock on the door brought him back to his senses.

You're a man of science, he scolded himself. And there are scientific ways to bring this nightmare to an end.

With cold, swift precision, he reached into his desk and pulled out a long hypodermic needle. Then he prepared a very special injection—one that would neutralize Josh's artificial blood . . .

And put the creature to sleep—forever.

He held the hypodermic needle into the air and studied the pale orange solution. There was more than enough to turn Josh into a lifeless vegetable. Then he stood up from his desk, and smiled.

"All right, Josh," he said. "Prepare to meet your maker."

Taking a deep breath, he walked out of the library, down the hall—to the front door . . .

Something was pounding against it, the heavy oak splintering apart with each infernal blow.

The nightmare had come home.

And once again, Grandfather Frank was forced to destroy the nightmare—like he had destroyed all the nightmares before.

A twinge of sadness filled the old man's heart . . .

Because every nightmare he created was the product of a simple and beautiful dream. A dream of life everlasting and death nevermore. But science was a slave to nature. The sleep of reason produced monsters.

Such is the way of progress, he thought bitterly.

Another earsplitting knock shook the wooden door in its frame. Grandfather Frank stepped forward and put his left hand on the bolt. Raising his right hand high in the air, he pointed the hypodermic needle downward—ready to puncture the creature's flesh when it burst through the door.

He was prepared for anything—a grisly confrontation fueled by all the fury, violence, and rage in Josh's soul.

But he wasn't prepared for what he saw when he flung the door open.

He gasped in horror and staggered backward. The hypodermic needle fell from his gnarled hand and shattered on the floor. His mind reeled in shock.

Two grotesquely gaunt figures stood in the doorway, their eyes burning with life . . .

Man and woman created He them. The words echoed in Grandfather Frank's head.

But these were no creations of God or nature. Nor had they been banished from the Garden of Eden, but from a garden of stone—Thunder Lake Cemetery. The stench of the grave rose up from their living cadavers, filling his senses and shattering his grasp on reality.

It's not them, he told himself. It can't be them. I

buried those filthy demons in the earth twelve years ago.

He closed his eyes and tried to banish the two visions of hell through sheer force of will. But when he opened his eyes, they were still there.

And they were walking toward him, into the hall, into the light, their faces worm-ridden and rotted—but still recognizable . . .

It was Adam and Eve.

And they had come to kill him.

Jessie heard the screams and dropped Baskerville's leash. The huge dog dashed toward the house, growling and snapping his teeth. And Jessie ran after him.

She stumbled up the stairs of the porch, gasping for breath. She paused at the doorway when she heard a chilling symphony of sound—barking, howling, shrieking . . .

And the anguished pleas of Grandfather Frank.

"No! Stay away from me! Nooo!"

Jessie braced herself and ran through the open doorway of the mansion. But she screeched to a halt when she saw the mayhem inside.

Both Adam and Eve had locked their huge, bony hands around Grandfather Frank's throat. He was lifted high in the air between the two creatures, and his legs kicked frantically beneath him. His screams of horror sounded like the hiss of a cat. And bloodcurdling laughter roared from the gaping, cracked mouths of Adam and Eve.

Meanwhile, dancing on the floor by their feet, the

dog Baskerville barked and snapped, nearly foaming at the mouth. His great jaws latched on to anything he could bite—living flesh or dead. The hound fastened his teeth to the father creature's thigh. The giant corpse glared down at the beast, then with a quick flick of his leg sent Baskerville flying across the room and into a wall.

Jessie screamed.

And ran to see if Baskerville was okay. She knelt down on the floor over the crumpled body of the dog and pressed her hand against his black chest. There was no heartbeat, no signs of breathing.

"Noooo!"

She wailed in rage. Then her head snapped around, her eyes burning with hatred. She glared at the two murderous monsters and shrieked at the top of her lungs . . .

"I hate you! I don't care if you're my mother and father! I hate you both!"

The two creatures turned to look at their daughter— and loosened their grip around Grandfather Frank's neck. The old man fell to the floor, coughing and panting, his face a ghastly white.

But Jessie wouldn't stop screaming.

"Why didn't you stay in the graveyard?! You're dead! You're not my mother and father anymore! I hate you!"

She pulled Baskerville into her arms, buried her face in his sleek black fur, and sobbed. She rocked back and forth, hugging her beloved dog—and heard the sound of heavy footsteps coming toward her.

She looked up.

And saw her mother and father standing over her.

Their faces were gray and lifeless—but filled with emotion. They looked strangely sad. And concerned.

Then the she-creature reached down with her long skeletal fingers—and touched Jessie's face.

Jessie knew in her mind that this hideous beast was her mother, whose love and affection she had craved for as long as she could remember. But when Jessie felt the rotted flesh graze across her cheek—and smelled the foul stench of death—she couldn't help herself . . .

She screamed like she'd never screamed before.

Sara froze with fear when she heard Jessie's shriek echoing across the lake.

She had nearly caught up with Josh, who staggered ahead toward the tall Victorian mansion in the distance—but the scream made her stop dead in her tracks.

She knew it was Jessie.

Sara's heart was racing. She had to save her best friend. But how? How could she stop two monsters when she couldn't even keep up with the one she created? Just the thought of it terrified her.

Then she heard something that terrified her even more . . .

Someone was running up through the dry weeds behind her, gasping for breath—and charging right at her!

She spun around, crouched down low . . .

And threw herself into the person's knees, knocking him to the ground with a heavy thud.

"Eddie! It's you!"

She pulled herself up and crawled toward the boy who groaned and rolled around in the weeds. Eddie clutched his right leg, wincing in pain.

"Darn it, Sara!" he gasped. "Why didn't you tell me you knew kung fu?! That's the last time I try to sneak up on you!"

"Sorry, Eddie," she said quickly, helping him to his feet. "Come on, we gotta hurry! Jessie's in trouble!"

She wrapped her arm around Eddie's shoulder and pulled him along, and he hobbled on one leg as fast as he could. As they rushed closer to the Frank family mansion, Eddie reached into his pocket, feeling for the remote control . . .

"Oh, good, it's still here," he said, limping up the stone path to the house.

"What?" said Sara.

"My secret weapon."

Bursting into the entry hall of the mansion—like a banshee out of hell—came a thing of violent fury.

The thing that used to be Josh.

He recognized the sound of his sister's scream. And he was driven by pure animal instinct to destroy whatever tried to hurt her. He stomped into the entry hall, roaring like a wild beast.

But when he saw Jessie with his mother and father, he stopped and fell silent.

The girl was crouched down in the corner, trembling with fear and clutching the lifeless body of the dog. The two rotted creatures stood over her, their quivering arms reaching out to her, beckoning . . .

Josh felt something stir in his heart—a strange glow unlike anything he had ever felt before . . .

His family was here, together. Home at last.

Then Sara and Eddie appeared in the doorway. Josh turned and looked at them, his eyes wet with tears. A gentle groan fell from his lips.

Sara whispered his name. "Josh . . ."

And he turned to look back at his mother, his father, his sister.

Jessie's eyes lit up when she saw Sara and Eddie. "Help me," she said softly, her voice trembling. "Get me out of here. They killed Baskerville. And they tried to kill Grandfather . . ."

Sara and Eddie turned their heads and saw the old man lying across the bottom steps of the staircase, clutching his heart and gasping for breath.

"Sara, Eddie! Run!" he wheezed in pain. "Get away from here! They'll kill us all!"

The mother and father creatures growled when they heard Grandfather Frank's voice. They turned around silently—and attacked swiftly.

Before Eddie and Sara could take a breath, the two beasts were on top of the old man, lashing at his face with their clawlike hands as he screamed in agony. Eddie fumbled for the remote control in his pocket. He found it, pulled it out, and took a step forward.

"Eddie, what . . . ?" Sara reached for Eddie's arm, but it was too late. The boy was just a few feet away from the rampaging monsters. He raised his right arm, pointed the remote control at the father's head—and pressed the pause button . . .

A wave of pain jolted through the creature's electrical circuits. A violent spasm surged through his body. It was almost as if he'd been switched off— like a common household lamp.

But the effect was only temporary.

The creature spun around with the speed of lightning and locked his hands around Eddie's neck. Eddie pushed the pause button again. The rotting corpse staggered backward—then quickly recovered, grabbing the boy's throat again.

Sara watched in shock as the mother tried to strangle Grandfather Frank and the father tried to choke Eddie. She looked across the room at Jessie, feeling helpless and terrified. There was nothing either one of them could do.

But then Sara noticed something strange . . .

A tiny spark of electricity flickered on a steel bolt in Baskerville's neck. His leg twitched, his tail flinched— and in the blink of an eye, the giant black dog jumped to his feet.

"He's alive!" Jessie screamed. "Alive!"

Sara gasped as the dog charged across the room and leapt into the air, his jaws clamping down on the father creature's neck. Eddie fell to the floor, his chest heaving, and the remote control flew across the room . . .

And stopped at Sara's feet.

Bending down and snapping it up, Sara pointed the remote control at the mother creature and pushed a button. Nothing happened. "It doesn't work!" she cried out, panic-stricken.

"Push pause," Eddie gasped.

Sara tried it again. The she-corpse twitched and fell onto the stairs next to Grandfather Frank. Then she was up again. Sara pushed the pause button. Once. Twice. Three times. White-hot sparks crackled out of the wires that pierced the mother's putrid flesh. She hissed at Sara.

Meanwhile, Baskerville had driven the father creature toward the front door. He growled and snapped and lunged—and both of them tumbled out onto the porch and down the stairs.

The she-monster screamed and staggered after her husband—out the door, down the stairs, into the darkness . . .

And Josh followed behind them.

Sara ran to the door and watched him—the boy she loved, the boy she resurrected—as he staggered down the stone path.

He was a lost orphan of the night, chasing the fleeing shadows of his mother and father.

He looked so lonely, it broke Sara's heart. She felt the tears burning her eyes as he disappeared into the woods, a tall, unearthly silhouette against the black shimmering waters of Thunder Lake. Then, with a single wail of despair, he was swallowed up by darkness.

Somewhere in the house, a grandfather clock chimed the hour—a slow haunting rhythm that reminded Sara of a funeral march. It was twelve o'clock. Midnight.

Halloween had begun.

16

Dance Macabre

From the diary of Sara Watkins . . .

Every day of our lives, we hide behind a mask. We disguise our pain, our heartache, our souls— with false identities as clever and deceptive as any Halloween costume.

Grandfather Frank insisted that we go to the Halloween Dance—as if nothing had happened. At first, I didn't think I could do it. But then I realized that I'd been wearing a mask ever since Josh killed himself. I was the great pretender—a skilled actress who had mastered the role of Normal High School Girl. It was, of course, a lie. But isn't life itself an endless circle of lies? We wear our masks to protect ourselves from misery, from loneliness, and from death itself.

But deep in my heart, I feared this Halloween would be different. Tonight, the masks would come off . . .

And death would show its face.

The sun hung low in the horizon, tainting the sky a deep bloodred. Then twilight descended upon Thunder Lake, changing the red to violet and blue. Mothers and fathers placed jack-o'-lanterns on their doorsteps and filled crystal bowls with chocolate bars and lollipops. Little children walked hand in hand through the streets—a tiny army of ghosts and witches and demons who frolicked in the night, frightening their elders and feasting on sweets.

It was a typical Halloween night in Thunder Lake.

But this year, the dead really walked the earth.

Sara locked the door of her family station wagon and stared across the school parking lot. She knew they were out there—somewhere. She could feel their presence.

Josh . . .

Her heart ached with longing. She closed her eyes and wished it were all a dream. Josh wasn't really dead. He was standing beside her, alive, and they were going to a school dance together . . .

Then Sara opened her eyes—and reality sank in.

She was alone. Her boyfriend had killed himself. And she was going to the dance by herself while Josh's resurrected corpse searched for his mother and father.

She felt tears coming to her eyes, but quickly blinked them away. She didn't want her Ice Witch makeup to streak. She reached up to straighten the white pointed hat with its fringe of plastic icicles. Then she smoothed out a wrinkle on the white strapless gown, took a deep breath—and walked into the school . . .

The graveyard was teeming with life.

Monsters and clowns and pirates wandered among the cardboard gravestones bathed in eerie blue light. A pair of ghosts in long white sheets fluttered up and down the length of the darkened hallway. And Death himself leaned against a giant cotton cobweb, pointing his scythe at a small swarm of bumblebee girls who buzzed through the crowd.

Sara didn't see anyone she knew. But of course, everyone was wearing a costume.

"Look! It's the Ice Witch!" someone shouted behind her.

Sara turned around and faced a ghoulish pair of bandage-wrapped mummies. The tall one wore a golden papier-mâché headpiece, like King Tut. And the shorter one wore a tall blue and gold crown, like Queen Nefertiti.

"Mike? Jessie? Is that you?" Sara barely recognized the two.

"I'm not Jessie tonight," said the short one. "I'm a mummy."

"And I'm a daddy," said Mike, grinning through the gauze. "You look great, Sara."

"Thanks," she said, twirling an icicle with her finger. "I figured since everyone thinks I'm an Ice Witch, I'll give them all the proof they need. I only wish I could turn some of them into snowmen. Then I could watch them melt."

The mummies laughed. "Come on inside," said Jessie, taking Sara's arm. "Your decorations look fantastic!"

They turned and walked to the entrance of the gym. A giant cardboard sign over the door read: WELCOME

TO FRANKENSTEIN'S LABORATORY (WE BRING BAD THINGS TO LIFE). And when Sara stepped inside, she couldn't help but gasp. It was like stepping into another world.

A green unearthly glow illuminated the morgue, the fake arms and legs reaching out from cardboard drawers—and looking all too real. A fiery red light shined down on a long table of macabre treats—candy skulls, cauliflower brains, a punch bowl bubbling with blood and eyeballs. The walls of the gym glistened in a purple haze of light, and the tall fingerlike shadows of gnarled cardboard trees and gothic window frames reached up toward the ceiling. There, high above the dance floor, a sinister cluster of blue storm clouds seemed to pulsate with silver lightning—a nightmarish illusion intensified by flashing strobe lights. But the most awesome decoration was the giant centerpiece that hung over their heads like an omen of doom . . .

The body on the lab table was covered with a white sheet. Suspended by aluminum foil chains beneath a fake electric tower, it was connected by wires and cables to a giant lightning bolt in the ceiling that flashed and pulsed under a strobe of brilliant white light. A long bandaged arm hung, lifeless, over the side of the lab table. Then—with an electric boom of recorded thunder sound—the arm raised itself up . . .

It's alive . . .

Sara felt sick to her stomach. It was all too grotesque—and all too real. She felt as if she were reliving that terrible stormy night—when she risked the wrath of heaven itself by taking matters of life and death into her own hands.

She looked down at herself through a veil of plastic icicles. She felt so foolish—for dressing up as the Ice Witch, for decorating the dance like Frankenstein's lab. But worst of all, she felt ashamed of her resurrected love for Josh . . .

I should be out there looking for him, she thought. What kind of girlfriend am I?

Suddenly someone whistled and everyone's heads turned toward the entrance of the gym. Sara looked across the room—and felt her heart about to explode.

It was Eddie and Kiki.

And they looked gorgeous together.

The redheaded cheerleader was wearing a short tight party dress that glistened with pale pink sequins. A diamond tiara sparkled on the top of her head, and sheer white wings sprouted from her back. She glowed with angelic beauty and grace. Sara couldn't help feeling a little envious—Kiki had never looked so beautiful . . .

And neither had Eddie.

He wore a crisp tuxedo with a pendant and a magnificent, flowing vampire cape. His long, wavy hair was shining, jet-black, and his eyes were like two fiery jewels that smoldered with hidden desires. He licked his full red lips and exposed two small fangs tipped with blood. It was hard to believe it was really Eddie. As a vampire, he looked so handsome, so dashing, and—Sara had to admit—incredibly sexy.

"Don't they look absolutely *divine*?" someone said behind her.

Sara turned and saw Heather Leigh Clark in a harem girl outfit. The sheer pink veil across her face couldn't hide the smirk on her lips.

"Hi, Heather," Sara muttered.

The blond cheerleader looked Sara up and down. "You look divine, too, Sara," she said. "You make a *perfect* Ice Witch. It seems so . . . *appropriate*. Anyway, I can't get over Eddie and Kiki. Who would have guessed they'd make such a gorgeous couple?"

Sara stared at Eddie as he held Kiki's hand—and she felt a sudden pang of jealousy.

"It was all your idea, Sara," Heather went on. "And I wouldn't be surprised if it turns into the latest school romance. Kiki likes Eddie a lot. She told me she thinks he's real cute."

He *is* real cute, Sara thought to herself. And sweet, and smart, and loving . . .

Suddenly a flash of bright light made Sara turn her eyes to the ceiling—just in time to see the fake body on the lab table lift its arm in the air.

It's alive . . .

A wave of guilt rushed through Sara like a jolt of electricity. Her feelings for Eddie betrayed her love for Josh. But how could she ignore her own heart?

She stared up at the cardboard lightning and the white lab table and the lifeless body . . .

And she remembered her promise to Josh—to love him and care for him forever.

She shuddered. Because she knew she had created an artificial life that would never, ever die.

And forever was a very long time.

She looked out at the dance floor. Jessie and Mike were dancing like Egyptians, their bandages rippling through the air. Kiki Austin was fluttering her fairy wings, and Eddie was waving his cape like a vampire bullfighter. Heather Leigh Clark danced from one boy to the next, from Jimbo (in a gorilla suit) to Crusher (in a gladiator outfit).

Everyone was having so much fun. But Sara could only think about the boy she resurrected—and his two monstrous parents . . .

Where did the dead things go on Halloween night?

The three creatures stared through the windows of the gym. They gazed at the flashing lights—at the lightning bolts, the morgue, the lab table, the thing under the sheet—and they knew they had seen these things before . . .

On the day of their creation.

The father, the mother, the son—each reanimated corpse remembered the horror of their birth, how they were wrenched from the peace and quiet of nonexistence and plunged into a hideous mockery of life.

Josh pointed to a figure on the dance floor, covered with bandages. It was Jessie, his sister.

His parents looked at their young daughter with love in their eyes—and fear in their hearts. Why was she wrapped in bandages? Was she, too, going to be hoisted in the air and turned into a monster?

This they would not allow. Their artificial hearts

were capable of human love. And like any mother and father made of flesh and blood, they wanted to protect her.

The creatures pressed their rotted hands against the glass and stared out at the crowds of young people . . .

They were monsters, all of them, in every size and shape. Zombies and scarecrows, witches and ghosts, skeletons and werewolves—a gruesome mob of monsters who defied science and nature . . .

Just like Adam and Eve and Josh.

At last, they had found a place where they could walk free, among the living, without suffering the outrage and terror that plagued them wherever they went.

So they staggered to the entrance of the school— and walked inside . . .

"I'm *dying* of thirst!" Heather Leigh Clark gasped, leaning on the shoulders of Jimbo and Crusher. "Let's get some punch."

She dragged the two boys toward the refreshment table and asked them to pour her a drink. Jimbo couldn't hold the cups in his gorilla outfit, so Crusher had to do it. As the boys fumbled with the drinks, Heather turned—and found herself looking into a bandaged chest covered with scars. Slowly, she tilted her head and looked up . . .

Into Josh's cold, dead eyes.

"Joshua Frank!" she squealed. "I thought you were sick!"

The creature stared down at Heather, its face gray

and haunted. A low grunt escaped its cracked, black lips.

"That's a *fabulous* outfit, Josh!" the cheerleader gushed. "So . . . *realistic*. You look just like the Frankenstein monster! It's *totally* creepy!"

Josh groaned and turned toward the dance floor. He was looking for Sara.

"We've missed you this year," Heather went on. "Poor Sara's been so lonely without you. She's even been dating Eddie Perez, she's so lonely."

She looked up into Josh's disfigured face, hoping to see some sort of reaction. Nothing. Just that cold, hard stare. Then he turned and walked away without even saying good-bye. Heather shrugged.

"Here's your drink, Heather," said Crusher, handing her a cup of bloodred punch. "What's up? You look like you just saw a ghost."

"Maybe I did," she whispered.

"Could I have the honor of this dance?"

Sara looked up into Eddie's gleaming eyes and smiled. "Sure, Eddie," she said. He took her hand and led her out onto the dance floor, where a slow song was playing. He reached around her waist with his right hand, a little awkwardly at first, then pulled her close to him. Soon the slow rhythm of the music took over—and they swayed in perfect harmony, like lovers who had danced together all of their lives.

"You're good at this, Eddie," said Sara, resting her head on his shoulder. "And you look absolutely gorgeous."

Eddie blushed—and pulled her closer.

"You're the gorgeous one," he whispered.

They moved back and forth, their bodies pressed together, the lights swirling around them. They could feel each other breathing. The whole world seemed to disappear as they danced.

"I love you, Sara," he said softly. "I'll always love you . . . no matter what."

Sara couldn't speak. She held on to Eddie as if her life depended on it. She needed him.

And yes, she loved him, too.

Crusher nudged Jimbo and pointed across the room toward the fake morgue. "Take a look at those two," he said.

Jimbo focused on the two tall creatures with wild hair and electrodes and worm-ridden skin. "They look kinda familiar," he said, squinting his eyes. "Is that Josh and Sara?"

"No, you idiot. Sara's dancing. And Josh is over there by the refreshment table. Don't you recognize them?"

Jimbo shrugged in his gorilla outfit. "I dunno. Is one of them the biology teacher, Miss Nevils?"

Crusher rolled his eyes. "No, gorilla brains. It's the crazy man and woman who attacked us in Thunder Lake Cemetery!"

Jimbo adjusted his gorilla mask and peered through the holes. "You think so?"

"I know so," said Crusher, lifting his Roman gladiator sword. "And I think we should keep an eye on them. Those psychos got us arrested. And I say, an eye for eye, a tooth for a tooth."

"What does that mean?"

Crusher ran his finger along the edge of his sword. "It means, we follow 'em tonight . . . and kick their butts."

"I don't know, Mike," said Jessie. "I've never been to Lovers' Lane before."

Mike pulled her closer and spun her around on the dance floor. "There's a first time for everything," he said with a grin. "I just want to talk to you alone, away from the prying eyes of Heather Leigh Clark and all the other local gossips."

Jessie smiled and closed her eyes. She hugged Mike Morgan as tight as she could, and felt emotions that she'd never felt before. To put it simply, Jessie Frank was falling in love.

"Why can't we talk here?" she said. "The party's hopping now. I don't want to miss all the fun."

"We can come back later," said Mike. "Let's just sneak away for a while. No one will even know we're gone."

The music swelled up, and Jessie felt a strange longing in her heart. Ever since Josh's death, she'd been lonely. She'd lost her mother, her father, her brother—and she needed to be loved more than anything in the world.

"Okay," she whispered. "Let's go."

Mike grinned through the bandages—and pulled her across the gym to the exit. The music faded behind them as they vanished into the night, two lonely souls looking for love . . .

But they weren't alone.

Two hideous creatures followed them outside.

And two boys, a gorilla and a gladiator, followed the creatures.

Sara looked up into Eddie's eyes.

And his love shined through, like a beacon in the night. She could no longer deny her feelings. Eddie was the boy of her dreams. Her Dracula. Her Latin Lover. Her Destiny . . .

So why was their love so cruelly cursed by fate?

Now—with the music playing, their bodies swaying, their hearts pressed together—Sara didn't care.

She lifted her head from his shoulder. Eddie leaned forward. And they kissed . . .

It was like magic. A beautiful spell that wrapped itself around them, lifting their souls higher than they ever imagined. Their love was the only thing that mattered. There was no such thing as death or pain . . . or monsters.

But there was a very jealous girl named Kiki Austin.

Without warning, Kiki grabbed Sara by the shoulder and spun her around. "Hey!" she shouted. "He's *my* date tonight! What do you think you're doing?"

Sara's jaw dropped open.

"Don't you have a boyfriend already?" Kiki snapped. "You're treating Josh like garbage!"

A sudden rage filled Sara's heart. "It's none of your

business, Kiki! Get a life!"

The fairy princess spit on the floor, then knocked Sara's witch hat off her head. "Oh, yeah, Ice Witch? You're too cold for one boy, how can you handle two?"

Sara screamed and shoved Kiki with both hands. And Kiki stumbled, tripped, and fell to the floor—crushing her delicate fairy wings. But she was up again in a flash, and fit to be tied. She dug her princess slippers into the floor and charged at Sara, knocking her down. In the blink of an eye, Kiki was on top of her, slapping Sara's face and tugging at her hair.

Eddie stared down, in shock, at the two battling hellcats. He couldn't believe his eyes . . .

They're fighting over *me?* he thought in amazement.

Sara kicked and screamed and ripped Kiki's sequined dress with her fingernails. Then Kiki grabbed Sara by the throat and started to squeeze. Sara could hardly breathe. She felt herself blacking out from lack of oxygen.

Then something unbelievable happened.

Someone lifted Kiki up into the air . . .

And hurled her across the gym, where she smashed into Heather Leigh Clark. Heather screamed. Kiki grunted. And both girls crumbled to the floor in a heap.

"What . . . ?" Sara gasped for air, and looked up at the silhouette that towered over her. It wasn't Eddie who saved her . . .

It was Josh.

And he was reaching down for her with his huge

gray hand. His monstrous eyes glowed in the darkness of the gym. His ghastly presence overwhelmed the dance floor. Sara hesitated, then reached for his hand. The giant creature pulled her to her feet. Then he turned and walked through the gym to the exit door—and vanished into the night.

Everyone was staring, but nobody moved.

Even Sara and Eddie were in shock.

And that's when the music stopped. The gym was silent and still, as if frozen in time. Then somebody screamed, and the strained voices of stunned teenagers rose to a deafening roar. It jolted Sara back to her senses.

"Come on, Eddie," she said, grabbing his hand. "We've got to follow him!"

Then they pushed their way through the crowds of gaping ghosts and ghouls and make-believe monsters, past the cardboard morgue, aluminum lightning bolts, and phony gravestones . . .

The monster they were after was real.

17

In the Shadows of Love

From a reader's letter in *The Coal County Daily News* . . .

To the good citizens of Thunder Lake: There is a place in our beloved town where innocent youth is corrupted by sin, where passion leads to pregnancy, and where earthly desire spawns eternal damnation. This place is often referred to as Lovers' Lane—but a better name would be the Road to Hell. And though it is paved with good intentions, the wickedness that calls itself "love" is surely the work of the Devil himself. So, I plead to the people of this community—turn your back on the idols of lust! Close down Lovers' Lane now! And lead us not into temptation . . .

—Name Withheld Upon Request

Mike Morgan steered the red MG through Lovers' Lane until he found the perfect spot—a shadowy cluster of trees with a view of the lake. He turned off the ignition, adjusted the radio for some romantic music, then unbuckled his seat belt.

"Well, here we are," he said to Jessie with a boyish grin. "Alone at last."

Jessie smiled uncomfortably and shifted in her seat. She was nervous. Her hands were sweaty, so she wiped them against the bandages of her costume. Then she looked out across the lake . . .

From here, she could see the family mansion, rising up like a knife in the moonlight. And farther along the edge of the dam, she spotted the old mill where Josh had been resurrected.

It seemed like she'd never escape the family curse. Everywhere she turned, something reminded her of the terrible secrets of life and death and monsters.

"A penny for your thoughts," said Mike.

Jessie frowned. "Oh, you don't want to know what I'm thinking about," she said. "It's too depressing."

"Try me."

Jessie took a deep breath. "Well," she sighed. "My family has had a lot of bad luck. My parents were killed when I was a baby. And my brother . . . well, he's really sick. Anyway, I feel sort of cursed. And every little thing I see makes me think about life and death . . . and other stuff."

Mike shook his head and stretched out on the car seat. "I know just what you're talking about," he said. "This car used to belong to my brother . . ."

"It did?" Jessie felt an eerie premonition of doom. She couldn't believe she was sitting in the car of Moose Morgan. And worse yet, it was parked in Lovers' Lane—where Moose met up with the creature that killed him . . . the thing that used to be Josh.

"I feel weird every time I drive this car," said Mike. "I think about Moose . . . and I wonder why he killed himself."

Jessie felt tears coming to her eyes. All the pain and horror and guilt of the last few months assaulted her senses, a whirlpool of horrible memories and nightmares.

The suicide. The resurrection. The murder. And now, even her long-lost parents had crawled out of the grave.

She buried her face in her hands and started to cry. She couldn't help herself . . .

And Mike Morgan tried to comfort her.

He put his arms around her and pulled her close, lifting the crown off her head and stroking her black hair. Then he raised her head with his hands and pulled the bandages away from her face.

Jessie felt exposed, naked, and ashamed. She didn't want Mike to see her like this.

But the boy didn't care how she looked. He wanted to feel her lips pressing against his. With a swift, sudden motion, he lunged forward—and kissed her.

Jessie tried to pull away, but she couldn't. Mike was on top of her, forcing his mouth down hard. She wriggled on the seat beneath them, and finally managed to break away from his kiss.

"Stop it, Mike. No . . ."

But Mike wouldn't take no for an answer.

He grabbed her shoulders with both hands and held her down, his lips attacking her neck, her face, her mouth. Then he was tugging at the bandages that were wrapped around her body, tearing them away as his passion grew stronger.

"No, Mike! No!"

Jessie struggled beneath him, her knees knocking against the dashboard of the car, her arms pinned to her sides. He was all over her—grabbing, squeezing, mauling . . .

"Stop it!!!"

He clamped his mouth down savagely over her open lips, muffling her screams. Jessie fought in vain. She couldn't believe that this was the boy she was falling in love with. He was an animal, a lunatic . . . a monster.

"Noooo!!!"

She managed to shout as loud as she could—but she knew it was hopeless. Mike was too strong, too crazed, to stop now. If anything, he increased the intensity of his attack, kissing and ravaging her like a madman. Hot streams of tears flowed down Jessie's face. She knew it was all over now. She didn't stand a chance . . .

Until someone ripped the car door open.

And wrenched Mike Morgan up and out of the seat.

Jessie bolted up and stared out the car window in shock. Two unearthly shadows held the boy high in the air between them. Jessie reached over the dashboard and snapped on the headlights. In the white glare of light, she saw her mother and father pulling Mike back and forth like a rag doll, as if they were going to tear him limb from limb.

She quickly slid out of the car and jumped to her feet, screaming. "No! Don't kill him!"

But the creatures ignored her.

They had seen what the boy was doing to their daughter. And they would never let it happen again.

They roared like wild beasts and flung Mike Morgan to the ground. The boy looked up in wide-eyed horror—and thought he was staring into the faces of Death itself. A wriggling nest of worms crawled in and out of their rotted cheeks. A blazing cold fire burned in their eyes. And their hands—their hands looked like skeletons, and they were reaching for him again!

Mike Morgan screamed.

And was lifted up high in the air. He kicked and squirmed and begged for mercy. But the creatures did not hear or understand his pleas. They carried him over their heads toward the edge of Thunder Lake, held him over the cold, glistening water . . .

And threw him in.

Jessie shrieked. She looked down to see Mike thrashing in the water, still alive, still screaming. His body was in shock from the icy temperature of the lake—his arms and legs seemed to be freezing up as he disappeared beneath the surface, swallowing a mouthful of water.

But the boy did not drown. He coughed and spit and flapped his arms madly. The blood flowed through his body, and he felt his strength returning.

He had to get away. Fast.

So he started to swim toward the center of the lake. He needed to get away from those . . . those *things*. He kicked his feet and picked up the pace, paddling swiftly and steadily away from the shore. But then he heard something behind him—a sound that made his blood run cold . . .

Two loud splashes in the water.

They were coming after him.

Mike Morgan swam and kicked as fast he could. His heart was pounding in his chest—so loud he could hear it. But it didn't block out the sound of splashing in the water behind him.

The two creatures were gaining on him.

He turned his head and looked back. They were about forty feet behind him—two demons from hell crossing the waters of the River Styx. Mike turned and looked across the lake. He fixed his eyes on the old mill on the edge of the dam. He tried to focus on that single distant point as he swam faster than he ever thought possible.

Soon he was in the middle of the lake.

But so were the two creatures.

One of them grabbed him by the ankle and pulled him under the water. The other one seized him by the throat and held him down in the icy darkness.

And Mike Morgan knew it was all over. He struggled as the monsters pulled him deeper and deeper—down to the bottom of the lake, into the blackness that was waiting there. His final moments were filled with terror. The creatures took fiendish pleasure in their tortures, wringing every last torment from the agonizing horror of the boy's drowning . . .

And Death, when it came for Mike Morgan, was a welcome relief.

Jessie stood on the edge of Thunder Lake with tears in her eyes.

She saw Mike and her parents disappear beneath the surface of the water. Then she waited—a long, long time—and tried to imagine the ghastly things that were happening on the bottom of the lake. It was too horrible to think about. Mike Morgan was being murdered, and there was nothing she could do about it. After a few painfully silent moments, she realized he was probably dead already.

She started to sob.

How could she go on living with a mother and father who killed to protect her?

If that was the meaning of love, Jessie didn't want any part of it. She wanted her parents to return to their graves—along with her fantasies of a perfect family. There was no such thing. No love in the world was worth the torment of murderous obsession. If anything, Jessie had learned to take care of herself. Even if Adam and Eve hadn't saved her from Mike, she would have somehow managed to survive—on her own.

There was a splash of water in the middle of the lake. Jessie looked up to see the heads of her mother and father breaking the surface. They lifted their arms in a gesture of victory . . .

And they roared in gruesome triumph.

The sound sent a chill up Jessie's spine. She looked out at the moonlit waters, rippling in cold silent waves. And she watched her parents swim away toward the old mill on the edge of the dam.

Mother . . . Father . . .

Then she turned around and stared into the blazing headlights of the red MG. Once again, the car was abandoned on Lovers' Lane. And once again, a Morgan boy had been killed . . .

Jessie sighed.

And froze when she heard a sound in the woods—the sound of heavy breathing. Her heart was racing, and she was afraid to move. Something was out there. She could hear it panting, moving across a crackling bed of twigs and leaves. It growled . . .

And pounced.

"Baskerville! Baby!" Jessie squealed with delight as the huge black dog jumped onto her shoulders and licked her face. "Good doggie!"

The hound panted with excitement, then stood on the ground, staring out at the lake. He bared his teeth and growled. Jessie turned and looked out across the water. Her mother and father had almost reached the other side.

She took a deep breath—and made a fateful decision . . .

Adam and Eve had given Jessie the gift of life, and now she would return the favor.

With the gift of death.

"Come on, Baskerville," she said, hooking her fingers through the dog's collar. "Let's go bury the dead once and for all."

Hidden in the woods of Lovers' Lane, Jimbo and Crusher saw it all—the monsters, the murder, everything.

They held their breath and waited until Jessie Frank ran off with her dog. Then they let out a sigh of relief. "Can you believe that?" said Crusher. "They *killed* him!"

Jimbo shook his head. "I tell you, they ain't human. They're zombies. And I ain't messin' with no dead things."

Crusher stared out at the lake, chilled by the thought that beneath the calm black waters, there was a corpse.

"So what are we gonna do?" asked Jimbo.

Crusher gritted his teeth. "We're gonna tell the cops," he said. "Maybe they'll believe us now, as crazy as it sounds. There are monsters in the world. And they've come to Thunder Lake."

18

The Revenge

From the files of the Thunder Lake Police Department, October 31, Halloween night . . .

9:21 P.M.   Incident at school dance. Girl claims "monster" threw her across the gym.

10:03 P.M.   Abandoned MG, red, discovered at Lovers' Lane. Registered under the name Moose Morgan.

10:16 P.M.   Jimbo and Crusher, suspects in the "crypt-kicking" case, claim to have witnessed a murder. Police follow up on report.

10:44 P.M.   Body found floating in lake. Identified as Michael Morgan, age 15.

10:47 P.M. Jimbo and Crusher arrested.
            Under suspicion for the mur-
            der of Mike Morgan.

The creature heard the police sirens in the distance.
It sounded like screaming.

He looked back and saw red lights flashing on the
edge of the lake. Crouching down in a cluster of
bushes, he watched the men in blue pull a lifeless
body out of the water. It was a boy, and he was dead,
but the creature felt no sorrow . . .

He felt envy.

Josh groaned in despair, longing for the death that
embraced the living like an angel of mercy. Dead
things couldn't die. Dead things suffered forever . . .

And they suffered alone.

Even his mother and father couldn't give Josh the
kind of love he needed. They were creatures far too
removed from life to understand his pain. They'd been
buried far too long. Now, freed from the trap of their
graves, they lashed out in anger and rage. They even
tried to give him the one thing he wanted most of
all . . .

Revenge.

But that pleasure would be his—and his alone.

The creature reached down below his chest and felt
the crumbled piece of paper he had hidden in the
bandages. It was his final message to Grandfather
Frank, a death threat that urged the creature upward
and onward . . .

Revenge.

He stood up and pushed through a tangle of thorns

that grazed his flesh. And as he walked slowly and steadily toward his destination, he thought about Sara.

She looked so beautiful at the dance tonight—a vision in white, glowing with life. And the way her face lit up when she danced with the boy in the cape, it brought tears to the creature's eyes.

She used to dance with Josh like that, when he was alive. She used to look at him in that special way that warmed his heart and made him feel loved . . .

But as the creature watched her spin and twirl in the arms of the dark-haired boy, he knew things could never be the same between them. Not anymore.

She would never again look at him that way.

And she would never again kiss him—like she kissed that boy on the dance floor.

The creature staggered through the woods, his tears echoing his sadness, and his sadness intensifying his rage.

Grandfather Frank did this to him.

He gave Sara the secrets of life and death. He urged her to rebuild him and resurrect him. He prolonged Josh's suffering beyond the grave—even after Josh had threatened to kill him if he did.

Revenge.

That was the one thought that urged him onward as he staggered toward the mansion on the edge of the lake.

Revenge.

It was the one thought that drove him down the stone path, up the porch stairs, to the front door of the house.

Revenge.

And it was the one thought that gave him the strength

to smash through the door like a human battering ram, stomping and howling, unleashing his torment in one shattering burst of fury.

He staggered into the entry hall—and looked up . . .

At the top of the staircase, Grandfather Frank was frozen with fear, like a deer caught in the headlights of a speeding truck. He gasped in horror. And he cried out in desperation . . .

"Josh! No!"

Josh's face twisted in anger, and it was a horrible sight to behold. Grandfather Frank spun around and dashed up the stairs, as quickly as he could, running for his life. He didn't look back—he knew the creature was behind him, reaching for him with those terrible, monstrous hands.

He flew up the stairs, past the second floor, past the third floor, and on up to the fourth floor—into Josh's tower bedroom.

The old man slammed the door behind him and threw himself against it. He expected Josh to pound and beat the door with all his strength—and he was not disappointed. The first blow knocked Grandfather Frank across the room. The door slammed against the wall.

And there, in the broken doorway, stood the final product of all his scientific dreams . . .

A raging monster that was going to kill him.

The old man picked himself up off the floor and held out his hands, pleading. "Don't kill me, Josh. It won't do any good. Please, don't kill me."

The creature took a step forward. And Grandfather Frank took a step backward, toward the tower window.

"Forgive me, Josh. I never meant to hurt you. I love you, Josh. I wanted you to live."

He felt his back press against the window as he moved farther from the approaching horror. He glanced out of the corner of his eye—and saw a small section of rooftop under the window. Maybe it was his one chance to escape.

"If you kill me, Josh, you'll live forever. I know how to give you death."

The bandaged beast stopped in his tracks, his mind spinning . . .

Death?

Yes, he longed for death—as much as he longed for revenge. Almost.

He took another step forward, his huge, scarred hands reaching for the old man's throat.

Grandfather Frank turned and unlocked the tower window. Then he started to crawl out onto the windowsill, but stopped . . .

Because Sara and Eddie burst into the room.

"Josh! No!" she screamed.

The creature turned and looked into Sara's eyes. They were filled with tears. It made the creature feel ashamed. He didn't want her to see him like this—filled with uncontrollable rage and killer instinct. He reached for the paper in his bandages—his final warning to Grandfather Frank—and held it out to the girl he loved.

Sara reached for the letter.

And Grandfather Frank crawled out onto the ledge of the roof, hoping to flee the nightmare he had created. He teetered on the edge, looking down at the stone path where Josh's body had fallen. But he was determined to survive this horror . . .

After all, he had survived many horrors worse than this.

Sara read the last line of Josh's letter out loud. "Resurrect me—and die." And suddenly she realized the magnitude of Grandfather Frank's crimes.

She took a step toward the window and shouted at the old man clinging to the roof. "Josh knew you were going to resurrect him! He told you not to do it! But you still went ahead and brought him back to life! And you made me do the dirty work for you! Why?! Why did you do it, Professor Frank?! Why!!!"

The creature snapped his head toward the window and growled in anger, lunging forward with his hands upraised and teeth bared, like a hungry predator descending on its prey.

Grandfather Frank screamed, jerked backward . . .

And fell.

Sara would never forget the sound as long as she lived.

It started with a high-pitched scream. And it ended with the sickening crunch of flesh against stone.

First, she stood there in a state of shock. Then she turned and ran out of the room, down the stairs, floor after floor, until she stumbled into the entry hall and out the front door . . .

Maybe he's alive, she thought. Maybe I'm being given a second chance to *save* a life, instead of resurrecting it.

She ran down the porch stairs and fell to her knees over the broken body of Grandfather Frank. His head was twisted back, his legs crushed. The stone path was covered with blood.

Sara had never seen a human body so horribly mangled.

Not since the night Josh killed himself.

She leaned over Grandfather Frank and studied his pale white face.

He was still breathing. Barely. And it seemed like he was trying to say something. His lips were moving, his voice a faint whisper . . .

"I loved . . ."

"Shhh. Don't talk, Professor Frank."

But the old man was stubborn. He wanted to speak.

"I did it because . . . I loved him," he gasped.

Overwhelmed with emotion, Sara began to cry. She saw the pain on Grandfather Frank's face, the torment in his eyes. And her heart went out to him, no matter what crimes he had committed.

"I'm a scientist, Sara," he whispered. "But I'm a parent, too. I only did what I thought best for my loved ones . . . my children."

The tears were burning Sara's eyes, running down her cheek and falling, drop by drop, into a pool of Grandfather Frank's blood. He closed his eyes—and for a second, Sara thought he was dead. But then his lips trembled. He whispered her name . . .

"Sara."

"Yes, Professor . . . Grandfather."

Slowly he opened his eyes and tried to smile through his pain.

"We're the same, you and I," he gasped. "We tried to create things . . . we tried to control things . . . because we're afraid of the unknown."

Sara felt a sudden rush of guilt sweep through her.

"Some things *can* be changed," he whispered slowly. "Some things cannot. And sooner or later, the things we create, Sara, don't belong to us anymore."

She lowered her head and began to sob.

All the feelings she had kept locked up—like wild things in a cage—came rushing out at once, flowing down her face in hot salty tears.

Then Grandfather Frank closed his tortured eyes, laid back his head—and spoke his last words . . .

"You do what you can, Sara. In this world, we're all on our own."

She felt his body go limp in her arms.

Grandfather Frank was dead.

19

Over the Edge

From the diary of Sara Watkins . . .

It's hard to describe the emotions I felt that night, when another human being died in my arms.

From the day I was born, I've tried to make sense of this world I live in. I've tried to define it, classify it, and explore it—like Columbus sailing across the great unknown to prove the world was round. But as the last words of Grandfather Frank echoed in my mind, I realized that all my theories were wrong. Some things cannot be defined or classified or controlled.

Sometimes the world is flat, not round . . .

And sometimes you fall over the edge.

Sara stared down at the lifeless body of Grandfather Frank—and whispered a silent prayer.

Then she stood up, her eyes filled with tears. Eddie and Josh were standing beside her, looking down at the mangled body on the blood-drenched path. Eddie reached for Sara and took her into his arms.

For some reason, the warm human contact only made her cry harder. She couldn't stop her tears from flowing—any more than she could stop the tragedies that had fallen upon the house of Frankenstein.

"He was a monster," Eddie whispered in her ear. "He didn't take responsibility for the things he created."

Sara looked up into Eddie's dark eyes. "But he was the only person who really understood me," she sobbed. "He understood my desire to control things . . . and my fear of . . . of being helpless . . . and alone . . ."

She started to sob again. Eddie held her closely and stroked her long blond hair. "Shhh."

Sara bit her lip and wept silent tears. She couldn't stop thinking about Grandfather Frank's last words . . .

We're the same, you and I. We tried to create things . . . we tried to control things . . .

She closed her eyes and heard his dying voice . . .

. . . because we're afraid of the unknown.

She knew those words would haunt her for the rest of her life.

Because he was right.

"I tried to create the perfect love with Josh," she said softly. "But I refused to let it die. Then I created the perfect friendship with you, Eddie. But I tried to steer your heart away."

She choked on her tears and pulled away from Eddie, ashamed of everything she had done. She buried her face in her hands, and cried.

"I'm like a smothering parent who loves her children to death. I'm no different than my own mother and father . . . or your mother and father, Eddie . . . or Josh's and Jessie's."

Suddenly a terrifying question crossed her mind . . . *Where's Jessie?*

It was nearly midnight, and Jessie had never come home from the dance.

Which meant she was still out there. Somewhere. And so were the two monstrous beasts that spawned her.

Whatever happened to Adam and Eve?

Sara's questions were answered with a sudden trio of sounds, three voices that echoed across the lake like music in the night . . .

First, there was the long, baleful howl of a giant dog—then, two unearthly shrieks that couldn't possibly be human.

"It's Baskerville," Eddie whispered, staring out at the dark waters of Thunder Lake.

"And it sounds like he's found Adam and Eve," said Sara. "Come on! I have a funny feeling Jessie's with them, too!"

She turned and ran toward Eddie's convertible. Eddie took a few steps forward, then stopped. "What about Josh?"

Sara froze, her hand on the car door handle. She looked toward the house, up to the stone path, to see Josh standing over the body of Grandfather Frank. His massive shoulders were hunched over, his wild hair falling into his eyes. In the distance, Baskerville howled again—and Josh lifted his head.

Sara's heart nearly broke in two when she saw Josh's monstrous face . . .

Because he was crying. Crying for Grandfather Frank. The man who raised him and loved him. The man who ruined him and resurrected him. The man he had wanted to kill.

And still, Josh mourned for his death.

Sara's eyes filled with tears, and her voice cracked as she called out to the creature. "Josh . . ."

Trembling with emotion, the monster turned his head and lifted a long, bandaged arm, reaching out for Sara.

"Come on, Josh," she said. "Let's go find Jessie . . . and Baskerville . . . and your mother and father."

The creature took a step forward, then another, his arms raised out like a frightened child seeking comfort and protection. He moved closer to the car, and closer . . .

"Now, wait a minute," Eddie stuttered. "He's awful tall. How's he going to fit in the car?"

"It's a convertible," answered Sara. "Put the roof down."

Eddie sighed and rolled his eyes. "Alright," he said, unlatching the convertible rooftop. "But I don't think my dad's gonna like it."

"He'll never know."

Sara opened the car door and took Josh's hand, helping him into the backseat. Eddie turned the key in the ignition. Then he glanced into the rearview mirror, his vision blocked by the hideous reflection of Josh's twisted face and sunken, glowing eyes.

Eddie muttered under his breath. "I told my dad

I'd be Mr. Responsibility. And now look at me."

The creature growled. Eddie stepped down hard on the gas.

"I'm driving a monster-mobile," he sighed.

Somewhere in the bushes, near the edge of the dam, Baskerville yelped in pain.

Jessie screamed—and pushed ahead, blindly, through a dark web of branches and shadows. She could hear the snarling of the two creatures, Adam and Eve. It sounded like they were killing poor Baskerville, tearing him apart, limb from limb.

"Nooo!!!"

Jessie cried out in horror as she burst into a small clearing. There, in the moonlight, she could see her mother and father crouching on the edge of the lake . . .

They were holding Baskerville down in the water.

They were trying to drown him.

"Let him go!!!" Jessie screamed hysterically. "Don't hurt him! No!!! Mother! Father!"

The gaunt corpses turned their heads and glared at their daughter. Then they released the struggling dog. Baskerville splashed and kicked in the water, his jaws snapping at the air.

He was alive!

Jessie ran toward the edge of the dam to help him— but froze in her tracks.

Because her mother and father were standing in front of her, reaching out with long, skeletal arms, trying to hug her, to hold her, to love her . . .

Jessie screamed.

And ran for her life.

She headed straight for the old mill, reaching into the mummy bandages to find the pocket of her jeans.

Yes! She had the keys!

She staggered to the door of the mill and grabbed the padlock. Her hands were shaking. She couldn't get the key into the lock . . .

And her gruesome parents were stomping down the wooden walkway behind her.

"Hurry, Jessie!" she screamed to herself, fumbling with the lock. The slow-moving waterwheel seemed to mock her as it turned and turned—cold and indifferent. Finally, she managed to get the key in the lock. She turned it. It clicked. The door swung open . . .

And Jessie plunged into the blackness of the laboratory. She fumbled in the dark. She tripped and fell. Then she scrambled along the floor in a crazed panic.

She had to find a place to hide. And fast.

Her mother and father were standing in the doorway.

"Faster, Eddie! Faster!"

Eddie turned the wheel of the car and swerved on the dirt path. Evergreen branches clawed at the windshield and scratched his shoulders. In the backseat, the creature howled.

"The mill!" Sara shouted. "Go to the mill! Hurry!"

He steered the convertible onto a smaller path and

headed toward the mill on the edge of the dam. It was just ahead of him now. He could see the silhouette of the waterwheel in the moonlight . . .

And he could hear the sound of Jessie screaming.

Josh roared in a thunderous voice—and lurched forward, crawling over the front seat like a rabid beast. He smashed against Eddie's shoulder with a heavy thud. The steering wheel spun out of control . . .

And the car crashed into the side of a tree.

I'm dead, Eddie thought. Dad's going to kill me.

He didn't have any time to worry about it, though.

Jessie let out a bloodcurdling shriek that destroyed any fears he had of his own father.

Eddie flung open the car door and jumped out. "She's inside the mill!" he screamed to Sara. Then he ran down the wooden walkway on the edge of the dam. Sara and Josh were right behind him, every step of the way.

But they stopped in their tracks when they heard something growling in the lake . . .

And then they saw something crawl out of the water.

"Baskerville!" Sara gasped.

The huge black hound pulled himself onto dry ground. His black fur glistened with water—and blood. White-hot sparks shot out of the electrodes in his neck. He bared his teeth . . .

And charged into the blackness of the old mill.

Josh staggered after him, howling and roaring in anger and rage. Eddie and Sara stood still for a second, frozen with fear. But when they heard Jessie's gut-wrenching scream, they rushed inside the old wooden building . . .

And into the darkness.

It's hard to say exactly what happened inside the old mill that night.

For Sara, Eddie, and Jessie, it was like being trapped in a nightmare so strange and horrifying that their minds were forced to erase it upon awakening—to keep them from going insane.

It was midnight on Halloween.

And the dead were restless.

Jessie felt their filthy claws wrapping around her body. Their bony fingers stroked her hair. Their foul lips touched her neck.

Eddie heard the savage attack of the dog—the snarling in its throat, the snapping of its jaws, and the tearing of flesh . . .

Sara felt the powerful arms of a bandaged creature embrace her and lift her into the air. She knew it was Josh, and she knew he was trying to protect her.

Then she was dropped down on the floor. Josh stomped across the room—and attacked the shadows near the lab table. There was a deafening crash. A scream. A roar . . .

And then, all hell broke loose.

Sara clamped her hands over her ears—trying to block out the bone-crushing sounds . . . and to keep her mind from reeling over the edge of sanity. She had never heard anything so savage in all her life. The unearthly screeches of four reanimated creatures bounced off the walls of the mill, filling her senses with a fury that was too primal, too brutal, to imagine.

It sounded like they were tearing each other apart.

Flashing white sparks blazed in the darkness as the monsters ripped out the wires of their own flesh and blood. It was madness, it was chaos. It was an all-out war of the dead.

And it was fought by a family that had been cursed from their first day of existence.

With a single, swift jolt, they crashed onto the floor of the mill and rolled toward the doorway, their hideous bodies silhouetted by moonlight. Sara cried out in horror. The four creatures were locked in mortal combat, their gruesome arms and legs kicking and clawing in a mass of rotted flesh. In Sara's eyes, they looked like one giant monster—Frankenstein's ultimate creation . . .

And they were trying to kill themselves.

Adam broke away from Josh and Baskerville. He roared and reached down for his wife, pulling her away, through the open door of the mill, and into the night . . .

Josh and Baskerville ran after them.

Sara felt someone grab her arm.

"It's me. Come on!" Eddie pulled Sara to her feet and dragged her to the doorway. But they stopped when they heard something behind them, in the darkness . . .

"Help me."

It was Jessie.

Sara and Eddie turned and ran into the laboratory, tripping over the fallen lab table. "Watch it!" Jessie cried out. "I'm trapped under here!"

"We'll get you out," Eddie said, feeling around for the edge of the table. Sara grabbed the steel legs and helped Eddie lift the table up—and off of Jessie.

She was sobbing as they lifted her from the floor.

"They killed Mike . . . They killed him . . . He attacked me at Lovers' Lane, and they drowned him . . . in the lake . . ."

She choked on her tears, clinging to Sara and Eddie like a child who just woke up screaming from a nightmare. They pulled her toward the door. She limped between them. And they all stopped dead when they saw what was happening outside . . .

Josh was crouched down over his parents, pinning them to the edge of the water. He pressed their rotted faces closer and closer to the massive waterwheel, until the green mossy paddles grazed against their worm-ridden flesh. They screeched in agony. Baskerville snapped at their feet.

And Josh forced their heads into the wheel.

The she-creature was the first to go. Her wild, maggot-infested hair was snagged up by a cracked wooden paddle—and she was dragged into the water by the force of the wheel, hissing like a cat, then silent. In a flurry of sparks, she was pulled beneath the bubbling surface—and disappeared.

Then Josh locked his hands around his father's neck and thrust his face into the churning waterwheel. A cluster of sparks and wires burst from the father's throat. Then one of the wires caught the jagged edge of a broken paddle—and he, too, was pulled into the water . . . and beneath the wheel.

Josh roared in triumph.

And the waterwheel turned. And turned.

Until Eve was lifted up, screaming, into the air, still snagged by the wheel. She was covered with green slime and moss. And right behind her was her husband, a hideous monstrosity that wriggled and kicked and bellowed in fury.

Sara, Jessie, and Eddie watched the spectacle in a state of shock. The creatures were riding the wheel, two living scarecrows that flopped back and forth, howling, rising up, up, and over . . .

Jessie cried out, her eyes filled with tears.

As much as she hated them—as much as she feared them—her heart was shattered by the horrible cries of her parents. They were trapped—trapped on the wheel of life itself, a wheel that turned and turned forever, without mercy, without relief, without death.

She pulled away from Sara and Eddie, and limped across the wooden walkway to stand by her brother's side. She looked up into Josh's sunken eyes . . .

He was crying, too.

The waterwheel kept turning. And once more, their mother and father were lifted up and over, in an arc of blazing sparks. Their decaying, bone-thin limbs twitched, and their bodies pulsated with electrical spasms. It was almost as if they were short-circuiting . . .

Or dying.

Jessie looked down into the channel of water on the far side of the wheel, expecting to see them rise up again.

But they didn't.

Their lifeless bodies were floating down the channel, bobbing in the water like dead fish—and heading toward the edge of the dam.

Jessie screamed. Because her parents were about to go plunging, hundreds of feet, into the darkness on the other side of the dam. She reached for Josh's arm, felt the stitches on his wrist, and held his hand. Then, together, in silence, they watched . . .

As their mother and father went over the edge.

20

Damage

From the diary of Sara Watkins . . .

It was a night of a thousand sorrows, a thousand regrets, and a thousand tears.

Tragedy upon tragedy had turned our world inside out. The hardships of birth and creation consumed us. The passions of mothers and fathers overwhelmed us. And the trials of life and death tormented us . . .

But somehow, we survived. There was no turning back.

The damage had been done.

Two headlights pierced the darkness like the eyes of a giant beast seeking shelter. And riding, in the belly of the beast, were five silent passengers . . .

A witch. A vampire. A mummy. A monster. And a dog with neck bolts.

They spoke not a word but listened to the soothing growl of the beast they rode, as it moved along the blackened shores of Thunder Lake, then turned up a dusty road and headed home . . .

To the House of Frankenstein.

When they came to a stop, Baskerville leapt out of the convertible and ran up the stone path to sniff the lifeless body of Grandfather Frank. Sara and Jessie helped Josh climb out of the backseat. And Eddie ran around the side of the car to check out the damages.

"My dad's going to chop me up into little pieces," he muttered when he saw the huge dent in the fender.

Sara turned and looked at the car. "It's not so bad," she said in a soft voice. "It can be fixed."

Eddie sighed and shrugged his shoulders. Then he helped Sara lead Josh toward the house.

The poor creature looked like he'd been put through a meat grinder. His bandages were shredded and torn and soaked with blue artificial blood. Broken patches of skin hung down from his neck, shoulders, and arms, exposing the steel joints and tangled clusters of electrical wires. The stitches on his left wrist were ripped, and the naked strands of muscles and nerves were throbbing from the pain.

But worst of all was the expression on Josh's face . . .

It was as gray as a tombstone—and haunted by shadows of such overwhelming sadness that Sara and Eddie could hardly bear to look at him. It was too painful.

They led him up the stairs and into the house, but Jessie stayed behind.

She crouched down over the body of her grandfather—and prayed for his soul. Baskerville sat down next to her. He pressed his cold nose against Jessie's neck and licked the salty tears from her face. She hugged him and wept.

"It's just you and me now, Baskerville," she whispered. "We're all alone."

She cried as she relived the horrors of her life. Her grandfather's experiments. Her brother's suicide. Her parents' resurrection. Her first date . . . ending in murder.

It was all too much to handle. She felt her mind shutting down, her heart turning to ice. She knew she had to focus on something concrete, something practical to occupy her thoughts . . .

Like what to do about Grandfather Frank.

Should we call the police? she wondered. An ambulance? A funeral director?

No, she told herself. They'll ask questions about Josh. Then they'll put me in an orphanage.

She sighed and wiped the tears from her eyes. Baskerville bumped his nose against her face, and Jessie squealed. "Baskerbaby! Your nose feels like an ice cube!" And then it hit her . . .

She knew where to hide Grandfather Frank's body.

Where the Frankensteins kept their most famous secret, hidden away in a block of ice . . .

The freezer, of course.

Sara and Eddie dragged the gruesome bundle across the basement floor. The white sheet was soaked with blood, and it left a long streak of red on the concrete. Jessie held the freezer door open, and watched in silence.

"Rest in peace, Grandfather," she whispered.

The body was placed along the far wall of the walk-in freezer. Then Sara stood up and pushed a strand of hair out of her eyes. She was exhausted. She glanced at Eddie, her eyes filled with sadness, and then turned her attention to the large block of ice on the shelf . . .

The frozen head of the original Frankenstein monster.

The hideous, twisted face and cold, dead eyes seemed to pierce her heart like a knife.

Why did I do that to Josh? she wondered.

She remembered the surgery she performed on his mangled body after the fall . . . the massive limbs of two dead football players that she grafted onto his torso . . . the steel joints and wires she implanted . . . the cybernetic heart she created—and broke.

Josh . . .

Eddie put his arm around her shoulders and led her out of the freezer, closing the huge chrome door behind them. She turned and looked at Josh, who sat in the corner and stared, in fascination, at the electric wires that pierced his broken flesh. He was crying, almost whimpering . . .

He was in pain.

The tears began to flow down Sara's face. It was almost as if she were coming out of a state of shock— and facing the night's tragedies for the first time.

Mike Morgan was dead. Grandfather Frank was dead. And Josh's monstrous parents were swallowed up by the darkness on the other side of the dam.

Jessie reached out for Sara, and hugged her. They sobbed in each other's arms—releasing a flood of anguish and pain.

"I don't care if Grandfather did bad things. I know he loved us," Jessie cried. "I'm going to miss him."

Sara nodded. "Me, too," she said. "He told me some things when he was dying. He said that he and I were the same. We created things . . . and controlled things . . . because we were afraid of the unknown."

"Everyone's afraid of the unknown," Jessie whispered, weeping. "I'm afraid of . . . what's going to happen to me. I'm all alone now."

Eddie stepped forward, putting his arms around the two girls. "You'll always have us, Jessie," he said.

Jessie smiled a grim smile and hugged them as tight as she could. "Thanks."

Sara rubbed her face, streaking the blue eye shadow with her tears. "Grandfather told me that some things can be changed . . . and some things cannot. But he never told me how to tell the difference between the two."

Jessie sighed, her eyes red and tired. "It's hard to say what's right and what's wrong," she said. "My mother and father tried to help me . . . by killing Mike Morgan. Maybe it was wrong. Maybe it wasn't. I guess we have no choice but to accept it."

"But what if someone else gets blamed for his murder?" asked Eddie.

Jessie looked at him. "That's something I can change," she said. "I can tell the police he was attacked by two people I never saw before."

Suddenly Sara broke down sobbing. Eddie and Jessie tried to hold her and comfort her, but she was trembling with emotion.

"That reminds me of Grandfather Frank's last words," she cried, her voice cracking. "He said . . . he said, 'You do what you can, Sara. In this world, we're all on our own.'"

The room was silent for a while—as the final words of a dying man echoed in the minds of three teen-agers . . .

You do what you can.

And with that single thought, they began to go to work—fixing the broken things that were within their power to fix.

While Sara and Eddie washed the blood off the floor of the house, Jessie went outside to hook up the garden hose. She stood in the front yard, her tears dried, and washed the blood from the stone path.

And that's when she heard the police siren.

She looked out across the lake and saw the flashing red lights of the police car, speeding along the lakeside road, coming closer and closer to the Frank family mansion.

Jessie was expecting this.

Sooner or later, someone was bound to identify her as the last person seen with Mike Morgan.

She took a deep breath—and organized her thoughts. She knew she would probably have to go down to the police station to make a statement. And she wanted to make sure she said the right thing, a story that would keep herself—and Josh—out of danger.

She closed her eyes and thought about her brother . . . her grandfather . . . her mother and father. And she knew she had made some bad choices in her life. But she also knew she was doing the best that she could.

Then she opened her eyes, walked to the end of the stone path . . .

And waited for the police car to arrive.

Sara watched from the window as Officer Colker questioned Jessie. The policeman listened and nodded and wrote something in his book. Then he opened the back door of the squad car, and Jessie climbed inside.

"He's taking her away," Sara whispered to Eddie, who crouched on the floor of the entry hall, scrubbing the streaks of blood on the floorboards.

Eddie stood up and peered through the curtains.

The police car's flashing red lights faded away into the darkness—and disappeared.

"She'll be okay," said Eddie. "She's a tough one, that girl. A survivor."

Sara nodded slowly. "Sometimes I wish I had her strength," she said. "Jessie has this great ability to accept things as they are . . . and to make the best of it."

"You're strong, too, Sara," said Eddie, placing his hand on her shoulder. Sara turned around.

"But I can't accept things," she said, her eyes filling with tears. "I try to change things. I try to control things. Just like an overpossessive mother who smothers her children with love. Like my own parents. And yours. And Josh's." She walked to the staircase and sat down. Baskerville rested his big black head on her lap, and she stroked his ears as she spoke. "I created the perfect love with Josh. But then I refused to let it die. And I created the perfect friendship with you, Eddie. But then I tried to steer your heart away."

Eddie walked to the staircase and sat down on the step next to Sara. "Remember what Grandfather Frank said? Some things can be changed. Some things can't. You do what you can, Sara." He looked down at the floor and blushed. "But I'll warn you now . . . You'll never be able to change the way I feel about you."

Sara smiled through her tears— and threw her arms around Eddie's neck. "You're pretty cool for a computer nerd," she whispered.

Then they kissed.

Sara closed her eyes—feeling the warmth and comfort of Eddie's love—and felt something stir in her heart. Something that gave her the strength to change the future, the serenity to accept the past, and the courage to go on . . .

"I think I'm falling in love," she whispered.

Eddie smiled, his long dark hair hanging down in his eyes. He reached up and wiped a tear from her cheek. Then he kissed her again . . .

And that's when they heard Josh cry out in pain.

He was down in the basement, but the tortured sound of his voice echoed throughout the house. It was a sound of great anguish—and great loneliness.

And Sara and Eddie knew they had to take care of him. First, they went to Grandfather Frank's study to find his bag of medical supplies. Then, they climbed down the stairs to the basement.

Josh was lying on his side, his giant legs stretched out over the splintered boards of the broken basement door. His long bandaged arms were wrapped around his torso, and he trembled like an animal that had been locked outside in the cold.

"Josh."

Sara whispered his name and began to cry. He looked so helpless, so pathetic—so wounded. It was almost as if Sara were looking at her own damaged soul, lying there on the basement floor.

But there was a difference. Sara didn't know how to heal the wounds of her soul—but she knew how to mend torn stitches . . . how to repair broken wires . . . how to heal injured flesh . . .

This was something she could change, a problem she could solve with a needle and thread—and a little compassion.

She crouched down next to the trembling creature and opened the bag of medical supplies. With a handful of gauze, she cleaned the wounds on his face, soaking up the artificial blood, sweat, and tears. She reached for his hand and studied the broken stitches, then pushed the wires and nerves gently into place.

Josh whimpered. He stared at Sara with eyes filled with pain, gratitude—and love. Then he opened his black, parched lips and sighed . . .

"Sa . . . ra."

Sara looked into his eyes. "I know, Josh," she whispered. "It hurts. But I'll fix it for you. I'll make it feel better."

Slowly and tenderly, she removed the broken stitches, one by one. Somehow, through her tears, she managed to thread a needle and sterilize it with alcohol.

Then, taking the monster's hand into her own, she began to repair the damage.

Epilogue

From the diary of Sara Watkins . . .

For the first time in months, I was able to sleep soundly—without grief, without remorse, without nightmares. Yes, I was guilty of crimes against nature—as guilty as Victor Frankenstein himself—but at least I was trying to take responsibility for my actions.

In my sleep, and in my dreams, the horror was replaced with a sense of hope.

But the curse of Frankenstein's children was not so easily put to rest. It reached out across eternity, trapped between life and death, and haunted us from beyond the grave. It lived and breathed inside Jessie's body, growing like a cancer in her flesh, tainting her blood and twisting her soul. It cried out to be reborn, in monsters old and new, real and imagined. But now I grow tired. I must wait another night to reveal the gruesome tale of Frankenstein's curse . . .

Now, I must surrender to the false security and

*comforts of sleep—and dream about the things I have
created . . . the things I have loved . . . and the things
I have lost.*

Tonight, I will not dream about monsters.

But I fear the monsters will dream about me.